De

Chronicles

Nathan K Fulkerson

DEDICATION

I want to dedicate this book to my wonderful wife,
Kristin. She has listened to me ramble and ramble
about this story for years and now it's finally finished.
Thank you for putting up for me and for all your help.
Without you I would have never finished it. I love you
so much.

ACKNOWLEDGMENTS

This book was originally written after I found out I had Dyslexia. I never liked reading or writing in school but when I started this story I fell in love with it. I found a passion in writing. I have changed the story a few times over the years but it is finally finished. I love to write and tell stories. I hope to keep writing and keep my passion going. Thank you to Kristin, Karlie, and Kaylie for your support. Love you.

Dean

"Why do we have to live here? I hate it here." I tell my mom while she works on some new project like always. In a town I have never been to in my life, my mom and dad have been working nonstop for the past three months. There isn't much around to keep a 14-year-old boy entertained in a lab full of older people.

"Honey, we are close to a breakthrough. You know your dad and I have to go wherever our research takes us, and right now, that's here." My mom always tries to find a way to make me feel better, but I still don't want to be in this drag town. There's nothing to do. Nothing. "Why don't you go play with the other kids? Veronica has a sweet little daughter that's close to your age." My mom smiles, as I roll my eyes at her. I don't want to play with a girl, and she's not close to my age, she's 9, I think. I leave my mom's office and go snooping around to see what carnage I can cause. I watch the research team in the different labs performing tests, and I play pranks on the security guards to pass the time. I know most of the people here hate it when I set off the fire alarms and screw with the camera, but I have to do something. My day still drags by even when I am being vicious. I see Veronica walking with a little blonde girl next to her in the adjacent hallway. She's short and thin, but she's very intrigued with everything around her,

1

unlike me, who doesn't want to be here, she looks like she's enjoying herself. I watch her walk down the hall and I notice that I'm staring at her harder than I want to or should be. She turns and catches me watching her and I jump back behind a column I'm close to and catch my breath.

"She caught me. Oh, my God. She caught me." I try to control my breathing and calm down. When I turn back around, she is still standing next to her mom watching me. She grins and covers her mouth giggling at me. My face feels hot and I begin to sweat as I watch her innocent face. She waves as they walk down the hall.

Holy crap. What was that Dean? I slap myself in the face and try to get a grip on what just happened.

The next couple of weeks I watch the girl play and walk down the halls, but I don't get close to her. I want to approach her, but I'm afraid to do so. She catches me watching her and her face turns red as I run from embarrassment. I always want to walk up to her and talk to her but I'm too scared to. Her mom even caught me a few times looking at her, I really ran then. Even though she is younger than me I still feel attracted to her for some reason. There's something about her that makes me want to talk to her and I don't know why. I've never felt like this before.

Ok, today is the day. I am going to talk to her. I tell myself that I'm going to make a move and see if her voice is lovely as she is. I see her mom and her walking, and I make my way toward where they are. *Hi, I'm Dean.* I keep saying in my mind. I don't want to open my mouth and forget what my name is. Finally, they stop to talk to someone in front of my mom's lab. I walk up to the sweet little blonde and catch a hint of her cucumber melon permeating the air around her. She smells intoxicating and I take a deep breath in to get my courage and tap her on her shoulder. She turns and grins at me.

"Hi, I'm Dean," I say as I take her hand and kiss it. I'm trying to pull out all the stops here.

"Hi, I'm-." Before she can say her name, an alarm goes off scaring both of us to death. I jump about five feet in the air and she screams as people push past us down the hall. Normally when alarms go off everyone looks to see where I am, but this time it wasn't me. The running staff members are heading toward my mom's lab and I turn to look through the window. My mom and dad are laying on the ground, not moving and the sweet little girl's mom is running to them. She waves everyone else away and the doors slam shut behind her, locking her inside with my parents. The little girl lets out an even louder scream and I cover my mouth, shocked at what just happened. A man grabs the little girl and whisks her to another room, but no one comes to take me from the spot I stand. I watch the emergency team finally enter the room after what seems like an eternity and take Victoria out, toward the medical bay. She fell next to my parents' minutes after the door shut behind her and without a protective suit on, she was exposed to what my parents were working on. But no one touches my parents. I knew at that moment they were dead. I scream and fall to my knees and that's when someone notices that I've just seen my parents die. My body goes limp as I am dragged from the area and someone takes me to another room. I keep crying and I want it all to be a bad dream. This can't be real; how can they be alive one second and dead the next. I can't remember the last thing I told either of them. Did I tell them I love them, or did I tell them how much I hate it here like I've done every day prior?

I don't know why I keep dreaming about my past. It's been ten years since my parents died and I'm nowhere closer to knowing the truth about what happened to them. I have tried to check on their research but everyone I talk to says that my parents were not on a breakthrough. I know my mom and know how passionate she was with her work and I know she had that look in her eye's weeks before her death. I pull the newspaper clipping out of the nightstand next to my bed. "Accidental death at Muller's lap." The front paper of the paper painted the story that my parents were killed by an accidental natural gas leak. The plant didn't have gas leading into where she was working due to the threat of it mixing with the chemicals being tested. "Dr. Mason's child receives two-million-dollar in the settlement." I set the clippings back in the draw. "Two million dollars." I laugh. "Like that's supposed to replace my parents."

I head to the gym to clear my head. I decided to take a later shift today and I wanted to blow off some steam. At the gym, it's time to get my game face on and kill my workouts. I channel my anger and hurt from the last ten years into every workout. I try to forget what I saw and bury the memory deep within myself. After the settlement, I thought alcohol would help but it only made me feel good for a day or two. After a few years of trying different methods, the gym was my outlet. Destroying my body and feeling the pain of my muscles growing was the only thing that seemed to help. I think all the time if I'm stronger, maybe I can deal with their loss better. I do large amounts of weights with high reps and try to push myself to the max every time. I put earbuds in and crank my music as loud as it can go. I don't like to be bothered when working out, and I don't like it when people recognize me and try to strike up a conversation. It doesn't happen that often though, thank goodness. But being plastered in the newspapers for years makes all kinds of people recognize you in weird ways.

I just did chest flies and when I start to work on squats, and I am feeling the burn on my thighs and butt. I gaze around the room and notice that a group of women are staring at me from the treadmills. When I make eye contact with one of them, she smiles and bites her lower lip, closing her eyes at the same time. The other ones smile and wave at me flirtatiously. I smile back.

"Can't I work out in peace for the love of God?" I say as my music blares in my ears.

I stopped spending so much of the settlement and started to save for a family one day, so right now I don't have room for a weight room at home. I wish I had just bought a new house with a weight room but Tony, the gyms owner cut me a break on the membership and cost, and I love coming to workout. Some weeks I come every day but most of the time it's every other day.

"Excuse me," a blonde-haired girl in yoga pants asks from behind me.

"Yes, can I help you?" I ask as I am taking my ear buds out. My play list is about two hours long and I was only thirty minutes into it when she stopped me.

"I can't help but notice how much you work out; do you teach classes or anything?" She says with a big grin on her face. "Private, classes?" She says as she bits her lower lip again.

"No." I say as I am drying my face with a towel. Sweat is pouring off my body like I have my own personal rain shower above my head.

She grins even more and says, "My friends thought you could come and show us how to work out."

"First, how do you know me? Cause I don't know who you are." I say, while studying her facial expressions to see if maybe she works in the same building with me or something. "Second, I don't think you want to learn how to work out."

"There was a lady that heard my friends talking about a party this weekend and she said you were in the entertainment business and that we would love what

you had." She smiles and looks down my body.
"And she wasn't lying."

"You have me mistaken with someone else. Yes, I
will teach classes on how to work out but that's it.
I'm sorry." I see she isn't taking no for an answer and
for some reason she looks like she doesn't believe me.
I think she thinks I do private parties for wild, drunk
girls. Maybe in a different life but not this one.

"Not even for me though?" She smiles and bites her
lip even harder this time.

"If you want to go on a date and see where things go,
then maybe. I don't know what kind of work you
think I do, but I'm not a stripper or something like
that." I say as I grab my gym bag from the floor.
"Excuse me ladies, I'm done for the day."

"I'll take you up on that date if you really want to?"
She smiles as I walk past her. I really don't care if I
ever see her face again. Pretty girls are a dime a
dozen in a coastal town in Florida. Even though I live
closer to Winter Haven just outside of my favorite
place in the world, Disney World, girls here are fake.
"Later Tony!" I yell as I walk out the front door.

As I walk through the parking lot toward my car, I feel someone tap me on the shoulder.

"Excuse me, are you David?" I turn around and a little old woman wearing the prettiest pink dress was standing there, looking up at me.

"No ma'am, my name is Dean," I say as I smile at her. I laugh to myself because I have been called David a few times in the past few months and I don't know why.

"Oh, you look just a man I knew years ago." She turns and starts to walk off but turns halfway back around. "Trust me when I say it's a compliment." Her wrinkled face smiles as she starts to walk off.

"Who is David?" I ask, longing to know what it is about this David that so many people see in me.

"David was considered a god back in the day. He was from Kentucky and was rumored to be one of the best male entertainers of all times." She smiles as she closes her eyes and takes one last mental image of David.

"I'm sorry ma'am." I apologize from someone reason, for not being someone she once hired for a good time.

"It's for the best. Heard he moved back to Kentucky and working at a hardware store." Again, she smiles as her mind sends her back to a time when she and he spent time together.

"Mother! Dear lord you scared me to death." A middle-aged woman yells as she runs up to the little old lady. "Are you ok?"

"Just thinking of him again."

"Mother, David isn't real. He never was. I'm so sorry. Did she stop you to see if you were David?" The little old lady smiles as her daughter scolds her for all to hear.

"She was looking for directions and I was trying to help her. Ma'am." I say as I nod to the old lady. She smiles as I walk past her and her daughter. I know she's not crazy because I have been asked a few times if I was this David guy before. Every time it's from older women and they all seem to remember a time, long ago, when times were simpler.

Heading back home I start thinking of what I just told that girl. Maybe she was just being nice or maybe she did find me attractive and wanted to go on a nice date. I laugh at the thought of a nice date. Most girls, if not all, want to go to a fancy restaurant and be pampered like a queen when they go out. I have the money to go to any restaurant I want to but why? I don't want to impress any of the girls I've dated in the past and I don't think that is going to change anytime soon.

"Is that even fair to her?" I ask myself out loud. I start to feel bad for her as I cruise down the road, just driving to clear my mind. I spend a little more time on the thought as I ease up to a red light as the sun tears through my windshield, blinding me temporarily. There is a minivan next to me with three kids in the back playing with action heroes and the mom is yelling on her phone as she holds one hand up to block the sun from her eyes. The kids look happy, even though the mom is screaming at the top of her lungs to whoever is on the phone with her. I try to remember what it was like to go on road trips with my parents as a child. They never screamed and shouted at me, but I always felt distant from them all the same. These kids though had each other. They're playing and fighting like I never got to on trips. All the trips we went on as a family were science trips that my parents loved, but I didn't care for too much. There was one trip that sticks out in my mind more than any of the other ones though. We went to Disney World as a family once when I was nine years old. Dad had won tickets through work and we were able to go to Epcot for the day. We spent all day learning about how their greenhouses made enough food to be used in all the Disney restaurants. After doing a back-stage tour of the greenhouses, mom and dad went to visit their laps where all the testing on each plant took place at. I never got to see any more of the park after that. It makes me sad to listen to her scream so loudly with her kids in the car though. I heard mom and dad fight from time to time but once I would come into the room they would stop. I was like they never wanted me to see them fighting. That was for the better though, their fights were on what chemical would react with what. I bet they don't even care their mom is screaming or they are just used to it by now. I can hear her loud voice over the loud roar of my engine from my supped-up Camaro. It wasn't the pretested car in the world, but it was my mom's when she was young. I remember going on long road trips with her and I would listen to the motor of the Camaro purr as we drove down the road.

The light finally turns green and the minivan speeds off like she has been at a drag strip, ready to win the quarter-mile race against me. It has been years since I dragged race and today was not the day I was coming out of retirement. I'm still dreaming of what it would be like to have a brother or sister to play with. Would my life have been different once my parents died, if I had someone to turn to? Before I can even let the clutch out all the way I hear a horn blow as a truck blow through the red light.

Memory

 "I can't take this anymore," I say as I pack my suitcase and head for the door.

"Where are you going, Dean?" Deloris, my foster mom, says as I walk out the front door.

"I don't know, but I can't stay here any longer." It's been 4 years since my parents died in the accident and it hasn't been easy to adjust to the new life. I don't have a family that could take me in and I'm too young to live by myself without a job. I finished high school, took an EMT class my senior year, and passed my boards so now I can get a job. I think I can take on the world at this point. Why not, the world has already delivered the first punch. I might as well stand up and keep fighting. I wanted to learn how I can save people since I couldn't save my parents years ago. I keep having nightmares of that day every night when I try to go to sleep. Deloris was nice, but she had six other foster kids at the house, and I had to share a room with two others, and I knew that I was just a paycheck to her. The longer I stay at the house the more money she makes off me. I have a settlement from when my parents died but couldn't touch it until I was eighteen, I'm ready to break free.

Orlando has a few places to get in trouble, but I

wanted to get into real trouble. I headed south to Miami and got a fake ID. I thought alcohol would help me forget my past or at least deaden it a little, so I tried it. After about twenty minutes a fight breaks out and some drunk lands on top of me, spilling my drink and pissing me off. I'm not in the mood for anyone pushing me around and I already had too much to drink for the night.

"What's your problem?" I yell at the drunk that is now grabbing my legs, trying to get to his feet. The other guy that just knocked him down is hovering over him, poised and for round two.

"Come on. You still think it's funny to hit on my girl." The drunk is trying to get to his feet and run for the door, realizing a little too late that he just made the biggest mistake of his life. He was messing with a girl whose boyfriend looks like a linebacker for the Dolphins.

"I think you taught him a lesson, why don't you back off?" I tell the linebacker as he glares at me. All I want to do is get back to my drink and the peace and quiet of the bar noise.

The drunk is finally to his feet and hiding behind me now. "Great!" I'm now in the middle of a bar fight that I don't want anything to do with.

"How about you move your skinny ass out of the way,

and I won't mess you up as well." The linebacker is pissed and has his sights set on me now. I try to explain that everything seems like a misunderstanding and he taught the drunk a lesson, so there's no need to kill him but I think the steroids have messed with his hearing.

Before I finish what, I'm saying the linebacker throws a punch for my face. I'm able to see it coming a mile away, even though I'm seeing double already from the booze. I sidestep and catch the mountain of a man in the side of the head with a right cross and he falls to the ground with a thud. I have never stood up to anyone before and I've never been in a real in my life. I've always gone to the gym in high school and worked out but that was just so I didn't have to go back home right away. The gym had a punching bag and I would spend hours taking my frustrations out on it. I never thought that one day I would actually use my skills for anything.

"Damn," everyone around says as the linebacker lays motionless on the ground. The drunk decides it's a good time to run off and I don't blame him. If the big guy wakes up, he's going to be one pissed-off dude.

Everyone's cheering and clapping for me, and the bouncers take the knocked-out fool outside to cool off. I feel pretty good about myself kind of like an MMA fighter that just won the heavyweight title. I feel like a hero.

"Hi." A blonde with long eyelashes is wearing a mini skirt that shows off her legs that seems to go on forever says. She has a tight tank top on that I think is her little sister's shirt but she stole it for the night out. I've never seen anyone that looks like her before in my life.

In high school, I didn't date and really never looked at chicks. I was always angry with my life because my parents and I didn't want to get close to anyone again. I figure if I never got close to anyone I wouldn't get hurt again.

"Hi," I manage as she steps close to me, clicking her heels on the tile with every step she drew nearer.

"I'm Roxanna." Her voice is a musical song, soft and sweet, but so sexy. I've never heard anyone talk with such a southern accent but yet still have a Spanish roll to her words. I can't help but smile at the way she makes me feel just by her standing close to me. "You want to go to the VIP section and *talk*?" She smiles at me as she reaches for my hand. I'm still not sure if I'm dreaming or if this is real. She pulls in her bottom lip and bites down on it as I feel sensations shoot through my body.

"Sure," I mutter as she leads me down a long hallway to a private room. Mirrors line the walls and ceiling

and there is a large bed in the middle of the room.
"This is the VIP lounge?" I whisper to myself.
Roxanna never takes her eyes off me as we walk into
the room, making me feel like the only person in the
club. She pushes me down to the bed and starts
kissing me while pulling at my shirt. I'm not sure
what to do, so I wrap my hands around her and kiss
her, but I feel awkward and clumsy.

Roxanna can feel my heart beating fast and my tense
body under her. She pulls me up to a sitting position
and straddles my lap. I look deep into her bright
green eyes and find peace. "Hmm," I say as I feel at
ease while gazing into her eyes. She is a complete
stranger and I feel the emptiness is filled since my
parents died.

"Have you ever done this before?" She asks as she
searches my face for the answer. I smile and look
down at the floor, not wanting to admit the truth.

"No." I say, still not looking at her face. I just know
the moment the truth is spoken she will be off me and
out the door as fast as she can.

She lets out a sigh and pulls my face to meet hers
again. "I'm going to regret this."
What does she mean by that?

"I'm a little confused." I say as she stands up
watching me and studying my movements.

"Relax. Trust me." I don't know what to say as she slowly moves her hips to the beat of the music filling the empty space in the large room.

"I do. But. I-." She places a finger on my lips and motions for me to be quiet.

She reaches in front of her and unsnaps her skirt letting it fall to the floor. She doesn't remove her heels as she steps out from the skirt and slowly pulls her tank top over her head. As I figured, when I first meet her I didn't think she was wearing a bra and I was right. Her stomach is flat and toned and her body is a sun-kissed tan. She only has on her sky-high black heels and a bright pink lace thong. She turns around letting me see her tight butt and she giggles at how much desire is in my eyes watching her twirl. She hooks her thumbs in her thong and slides them down her long legs, with her back to me. Bending over at the waist as she reaches her heels. She kicks it to the corner of the room and walks back over to me. Pulling me up from the bed, she slowly pulls my tee-shirt over my head.

"Wow, wasn't expecting that." She says as she runs her hand down my chest and my abs. "Do you work out every day? Your body is rock hard." I've never thought of my body looking good, I knew that I had a good six-pack and toned chest but I'm not bulky at all. I love how she can't keep her hands off my chest and stomach though.

As her hands slid down my abs to my pants she goes to her knees, kissing my six-pack as her hands to take my pants off, leaving my boxers on. I feel embarrassed to sit in front of her gorgeous body only wearing my boxers while she is only in heels. She hooks her hands in my boxers and pulls them down. My heart races as now I am in front of a girl for the first time with nothing on.

"Good Lord." She exclaims, licking her lips. Her small, well-manicured fingers trace a line down my abs.

"Oh! Oh!" I try not to scream, but I've never felt anything like this before. She grins at my moans as she kisses me. She stands up and tells me to get on the bed. Reaching in a drawer that's next to the bed, she pulls a wrapper and rips it with her teeth pulling out a condom for me. She helps me put it on since I have never worn one before in my life. I can't believe this is happening to me and I close my eyes, trying to relax my body as I feel her straddle my legs as she makes her way to my waist.

"Relax and let me do everything." She says as she hovers over me. She slowly lowers herself down onto me, squeezing my hips with her thighs as she takes me deep inside her. I can feel the ring that is in her rub against me as she moves deeper on me. "Oh!"

She lets out a scream as she pushes me as deep as she can. She is warm and wet, and her thighs are soft against my skin. She runs her hands down my chest to my abs holding my sides as she rocks back and forth. I close my eyes and took a deep breath, smelling the cheery lip gloss she's wearing and a hint of lavender. She rocks and moans as she pulls and claws at chest and abs as she works her hips deeper. I push back on my elbows and set up to her as she wraps her arms around my back. Digging her French tip nails into my skin. I want to kiss her, but I'm not sure if I'm supposed to. Are there rules for what I can do or not do? I'm so confused and she senses my conflict inside me as she grasps the back of my head and slams her mouth against mine. Parting my lips with her skilled tongue, she dances in my mouth for a few minutes.

Her heels are digging into my side as she rocks harder on me. I can't believe how long sex takes, and I'm not sure what's supposed to happen at the end. Would I know when it's over? I only knew what it's like to be alone for so many years and this is much better. Much, much better. She pulls her mouth away from mine and throws her head back, screaming and cruising as she slams her body repeatedly against mine. Her screams grow louder as she digs deeper into my back with her nails. I open my mouth as I feel the release of pressure starts and finally ends in the condom. We both let out a scream and she pulls my head to her chest, making me bury my head and face on her.

I knew that's the end and I'm no longer a virgin. *My God did that feel good.*
She holds me tight to her body for a few more minutes, until my breathing calms down and my body is no longer jerking. My muscles are tense and I feel like I've been in the gym for hours, but it's only been twenty minutes.

"How do you feel now?" She asks as she rolls off my body onto the bed.
"Words can't explain it. Wow." I say, looking at her, still panting like a dog.

"You should really use that sexy body of yours for this more often. Do you want a job?" What is she asking? If I want a job having sex?

"I don't have a job or anything, but what are you talking about exactly?"
"I know a man named Lorenzo that owns and runs a club, I think you would make a great addition to his team. If you want, you can have this every night." She licks her tongue up my cheek to my ear as she whispers the last part.

Dean

My brain starts to work in overload after I feel the recent memory I had of Roxanna slipping. "Why are you in my head?" I ask out loud, as I notice the large pickup truck with four doors, slamming into the side of the van. The mom's neck snaps instantly as the truck plows through the side of the van and the kid's action heroes go flying out of their hands. I am still sitting at the light, not believing what I'm seeing. One minute the kids are talking, laughing and having fun in the back of the van and the next they're violently thrown around as the truck grinds to a halt into their side. The truck burst into flames as soon as it comes to a stop and I see the driver jump out and run for cover. Everyone else around the accident is in shock as the truck is turned into an inferno of twisted metal while it's buried deep into the van. I step out of the car and look at the vehicles while I hear someone yell, "Call 911." Then another person says, "There are kids in the van, they can't get out."

Without thinking for my own safety, I run to the van, pushing people out of my way as I go. One guy yells for me to wait for the fire department before I kill myself.

Waiting isn't an option and I know what needs to be done to save the kids. I run to the back of the van and break the rest of the back window out with my hand. trying to clear a spot so I can climb through. As I fall inside the van, I feel the intense heat from the truck hitting me like I'm in a lava pit. The kids start screaming and yelling as they are fearing they are going to be cooked alive. I'm able to break two of the seat belts free and lift the boys up and out the window I busted out. The same guy that was yelling for me to stop is now waving for the boys to come to him for safety. Douche bag wants to be the damn hero hoping that someone gets it on video of him running to safety with the boys. Look at me, I'm the hero of the day, I saved these boys. I think in my head as I watch the boys run from the terror that just replaced their evening. "God, I hate people sometimes." I say under my breath as I see Mr. Douche smile as he takes them to safety, practicing his grin for the news team when they do arrive. The girl on the other hand is pinned from the force of the truck and it takes me a little longer to free her. I'm able to get her seat belt off but I'm not able to free her leg from the side of the van. "Can you move, any?" I ask her as I frantically look for a solution to free her. My brain is working in overdrive as I know the fire is raging out of control just feet from where she is at.

"No," she screams as she starts to cry. "No, I'm stuck!" She screams more as the heat in the van is starting to feel like the inside of a volcano. "I don't want to die." She repeats.

"Listen, I'm a trained EMT and I am not leaving you until I free your leg." I say, trying to reassure her that she'll be ok. I've never used my skills but it's like riding a bike, once I start searching my mind for the answer for what to do, it's right in front of me. I know that I was told time and time again to make sure the scene is safe before entering, but I'm not about to watch someone burn alive when I have a chance to save them. I know what I need to do and how to do it as I look in the little girls eyes. "On the count of three I am going to try and push this metal away from your leg, when I do, I need you to pull your leg out. It's going to hurt and it's going to be hot." I tell her as I reach down to push the metal. The metal is scorching hot and the paint is starting to peel off the van from the heat of the fire. The window above her head is melting and the flames are getting larger. I know that at any moment the truck's gas tank is going to explode, and we will both be dead.

I start to count, "One," the heat is making me sweat so much I can't get a good grip, "Two." The metal is so hot now my fingertips are turning red. "Three," I yell and push with all the strength I have. The girl's leg comes out of the twisted metal and blood pours out a large gash in her leg. I throw her up and out of the window of the van onto the pavement. I hear the fire roaring behind me and then the flame sucks back into the truck like it just took a deep breath. Everyone is yelling for me to get out of the way as I land on the ground and grab the girl in my arms and start running as fast as I can. I can't make out what the crowd is yelling as I keep thinking about whether or not, I will save her.

"I will save her." My mind is screaming as the truck explodes, throwing pieces of metal everywhere. The van is forced back from the truck like it was on a landmine as the shockwave slams my body to the ground. I can see flashing lights, but I can't hear anything. The weight of the girl is lifted off my arms and someone is dragging me to the side of the road.

I wake up lying in a hospital bed somewhere in Orlando, but I have no clue where I was taken to or how I got there.

A slow, steady knock on the door wakes me up. "Come in," I say as I set up, unable to move much.

Two police officers walk in the room, one a male, six-foot plus and very muscular. The other is a female, a little over five foot tall with her hair pulled back and trying to hide her smile as they walk through the door. "Dean?" The male officer asks.

"Yes, what can I do for you?" I say with a confused look on my face.

"Sir, did you see the accident today? Are you aware that someone died because of that accident?" He says in a deep, demanding voice.

"Yes," I say as I set up a little more, "I saw a truck run the red light and hit a van in the side. I noticed the driver of the truck run once it caught fire and I also noticed that the woman in the front seat was dead upon impact or at least it looked like she was dead." I finally make it to a full sitting position and suck in a deep breath.

The male officer extents his hand, "Thank you for stepping in and saving those kids, you should be very proud and your family should be also."

"Thank you sir," I say and he turns and starts out the door.

The female officer leans in close to give me a hug and whispers, "I would love to think you in my own way." She lets her hand slid across my chest as she smiles and winks as she walks out of the room.

"I just did what anyone would have done." I laugh as I feel a sense of pride fill my body. "Nice way to pick up chicks Dean." I say as I look down at the bruises littering my body. "Nice, painful way."

"Dean, how are you feeling today?" A skinny blonde interrupts my self-loathing as she enters the room wearing tight scrubs. Her hair is golden and pulled back into a ponytail. She's wearing dark-rimmed glasses with a hint of lip gloss shimmers as she grins.

"You look familiar. Do I know you?" I keep studying her face, but I can't put a name with it or remember where I've seen her before.

"You don't remember me if I'm not in yoga pants, and hitting on you while you work out?" She giggles as I start to blush a little.

Great, my mind slaps the back of my head. I hope she was offended when I blew her and her friends off the other day. The worst part is, I've been out of it for three days so no telling what I've said or done in that time.

"I'm glad to see you're feeling better." She starts to take a blood pressure when she stops and looks at my body.

I sheepishly grin and try to cover up but she grins and finishes taking my blood pressure. "Good to see that gym shit really does work."

She finishes checking my vitals and charting on the computer before turns to leave. "I'll check on you later. If you need anything, and I do mean anything," she bites her bottom lip. "I will take care of you, I promise."

"Thank you." I manage before she walks out the door. "I love this hero stuff."

I call work and tell them what happened to me and that I am still in the hospital for a few more days. They tell me to take the rest of the week off and come back when I'm feeling better.

I stay another two days in the hospital and talk with the nurse. I gave her some workout advice and we exchanged numbers before I was released. I might call her but most likely I won't.

I go to the police station and pick my car up. Apparently, someone drove it there were no one would steal it. I'm glad they did.

"Hi, I'm here to pick up my car." I say to the officer behind the window at the impound lot.

"Name?" He asks as he pulls open a new page on his computer. He's a big guy with a rough face. It looks like he's mad that he is working behind a desk and not like most people that are mad just to be working. His thick neck tells me he was a weight lifter and he probably worked vice unit or something before being assigned the impound yard. I see scars on his arms and face from years of close calls and his voice is deep and demanding. But it ached with each syllable he made. He doesn't want to be here and it shows. He probably was hurt in the line of duty and is now forced to take a desk job, which he dislikes with a passion.

"Dean." I say, "Dean Mason." The name didn't flow off my tongue very easily. I only go by Dean and never by my last name after my parents died. I never use my last name anymore and hate that it reminds me of them. Most people know me as Deano.

"Here we go Mr. Mason, I found you." His voice commands.

"It's just Dean." I interrupt.

"Sure," the officer says. "Sign here Mr. Mason and here are your keys." He hands me my key chain that only has three keys on it, my car key, my house key, and door key for work. "Have a good day Mr. Mason." The officer sits back down and starts reading his paper again, he doesn't look up at me again and never smiles as he sits there.

"I think he's ready for retirement to kick in and go home." I laugh as I walk toward the car.   "At least, he was nice." I jokingly say as I make my way to the car.

After my week off from work, it was time to get back at it. A few years ago, I found a job working in pharmaceuticals and it paid great. The only bad thing about the job was the slimy ass for a boss I had.

It was day in and day out the same routine. I thought when I accepted this new position with Muller Pharmaceuticals, I would be making a difference in the world. I found out last week that the ones that make the real difference in the world are the first responders that save lives every day without a second thought of their actions. After three painfully long, tiresome years making some corrupt stiff millions of dollars, I'm ready to quit. My mom always told me to never quit or give up on my dreams, but this isn't my dream. I thought I could follow in her footsteps some and see what drew her so passionately to work with pharmaceuticals. She and my dad meet one day when they were working in sales and from there, they both went back to school and received their PhDs. I wasn't planned and took both of them by surprise, but they loved me all the same. Their jobs were demanding, and it took them all over the world at times, but they always had time for me. I felt like a lot of time that I was in the way and hindered their research, but I know they were just consumed with their work.

Dean

I walk up to the front door and admire the large glass all around the opening. For a research and development company, Muller's had the look of a fortune 500 place. I guess that's what Mr. Muller was going for in the design. Through the large glass door, I notice a few ladies working on computers and typing away while going through large stacks of papers. "I'm I in the right place?" I ask myself. When I left a week ago, there was nothing in the front lobby except the security desk. What's going on? My mind raced as I pushed through the door. It opens a lot heavier than it looks and a set of chimes go off alerting everyone to my presence.

"What the hell?" I exclaim. All the ladies look up, without missing a keystroke, and greet me. "Good morning," A one-tone, unison-like chant says. "How may we help you?" The closest one to me said with a big smile on her face.

"I work here? I think?" I question as I adjusted my shirt making sure everything is still tucked in and I look proper. I'm thinking of how odd it is that everyone in the building is so happy and joyful to be working. It wasn't like that when I left.

"Hi, my name is Gloria." A woman says as she comes out from one of the back offices wearing a pinstriped suit and with blonde hair that is up in a bun. Her words roll off her tongue with ease about them. I can tell she's not American, but I'm not sure yet where she's from. She looks like a woman that's been working in a man's world and one that knew how to handle herself very well. She's slender and tall, but I can tell she's toned and that she works out. Probably a yoga junky, not a gym girl. Her shoulders aren't broad, but she has definition in her arms and neck. When she walks, her arms don't sway as she keeps them close to her in a defensive posture.

I extend my hand to her, "Hi, my name is Dean." She shakes my hand and I'm surprised at how strong of a grip she has. Not trying to be sexist but for a woman, she has one hell of a grip.

"Follow me please, we've done some remolding." Her accent is bothering me because I can't place it off-hand. She has a German style of speaking, real harsh and direct, but it has a roll to it that makes me lose all train of thought. It's majestic and strange, something that I've never experienced before. Living in South Florida. you hear a lot of accents, mainly a ton of Spanish, or some form of Spanish. So, this really sticks out to me. It's beautiful though, I'm hanging to every syllable as she speaks.

"I'm sorry, can you repeat the question?" I'm lost in her voice and her face as I watch her mouth make these sounds of beauty. My mind keeps going to other places. For once I'm just lost in thought. I'm impressed. Impressed that she's so well-spoken and direct with every question, I feel like I'm in the twilight zone.

"I asked, what job do you do now?"

"Well," I grin as I think of how to explain what I do for the company. "Right now, I set up meetings with new clients in hospitals, doctors' offices, or any other medical aspect for them to sample our top products. Most of the time I am on the phone, scheduling appointments for them to try our products out. I have worked in the lab some and love seeing how each drug is made and what effects it has on the human body.

"I'm not sure if you will be doing the same job again or something new." She motions for me to enter an office. "Wait here and I will be right back."

"What the hell is going on?" I ask myself she steps out of the office and I can hear her heels clicking down the hall.

I wait for what seems like forever until Gloria returns with another woman. She is

"Dean," I hear a soft voice say, right before I enter the room.

"Yes." I turn around and see Gloria standing in a doorway motioning for me to come to her. I walk into the room where she is and find her standing with the goddess I keep seeing at the club. The woman that Gloria said was her boss.

"Dean," Gloria motions for me to sit down. "This is Gabriela. She is the boss and sort of, owner, of the company."

"Hi." I swallow hard and try to come up with more words than just, HI. No words are making their way up to my mouth though as I stare at her beauty. I'm mesmerized by her sexy, slim body. She's wearing a tight dress that comes right above her knees and a small strapped top with a jacket on. Her long legs are crossed and she's showing off the red soles of her heels. There is no doubt she has money and she doesn't care to show it.

"I am a little confused." I say, finally being able to speak. "What am I doing here and why aren't I back at my station working?"

Gloria turns and looks at me, "We are changing some aspects of the company."

"That shouldn't make a difference with me though." I interrupt, trying to explain my side of things.

Gloria holds her hand up to stop me from saying

anything more. "Listen. We know you have worked here for a while now, but we are going in a new direction now."

"What the hell are you saying?" I demand as I search both of their faces.

"We are letting you go." That thick accent rolls off Gabriela's tongue and hits me like a freight train to the face. I sink back into my chair as her and Gloria stares at me.

"Why the FUCK?!" I want to say more but Gabriela stands up and cuts off my words with the palm of her hand.

"Dean, I am sorry. I truly am, but we are moving forward, and you are not in the plan to move forward with us." Gabriela is now standing in front of me, almost in my lap as she stands tall, posed for the next words that come out of my mouth.

"But why?" I know she just told me why she is letting me go, but for some dumb reason, I want to keep hearing her speak.

 Her dress is tight against her skin and she makes it harder to think straight.
"Dean, don't make this harder than it is. You seem like a nice guy and all." I try to interrupt but Gloria hands me a letter of termination and a check for

$80,000 dollars. "This is close to what you would have made by the end of this year. If you need help finding another job just let us know but for now, please don't come back." Gloria gives me a business card with her cell phone number on it and motions for me to leave.

"I don't agree with you." I turn around, pissed off at what just happened. "I don't agree with you one bit. I don't understand why I am getting fucking fired after I have worked for the last three damn years for this fucking company." I want to say more but the security guard steps into the door and motions for me to walk with him. "Piss on you!" I yell at him. As I start out the door, I hear Gabriela and Gloria whispering to each other. I start out the door and hear the two women talking to each other.

"He has no idea, does he?" Gabriela asks Gloria. "He didn't have time to meet her, did he?"

"I think we caught him in time, just make sure to keep her away from him and he will never find out." Gloria snarls.

I take a drive to cool my head before heading home. I feel like shit, but I really don't know why. I was planning on quitting soon anyway if I didn't find any more out on the drug my parents were working on. I thought the records from their work would be in the archive room, but I haven't been able to make my way there with all the security. I rub my neck and with my palm as I turn down my street. I text the nurse I met the other day to see what she was up to tonight. I wasn't expecting her to text me back, but she responded very quickly. When I pull into the drive, she is sitting on the front porch waiting on me. I didn't realize how she looked when we were at the gym but she has short blonde hair and today it is not pulled back into a ponytail. She is wearing short purple shorts that show off her long legs and notice how to tone her legs are. She has a baggy shirt on that comes down about as far as her shorts come down, which is not long at all. Her shirt has a yoga symbol on that I have no clue what it means but she looks very cute. She doesn't look like she is wearing a lot of makeup and she gins as I step out of the car.

"Hi." Her cheeks turn red as I walk to the front porch.

"Hi yourself." I laugh at how simple she seems as I take the air up between us.

"I'm happy you called." I shrug my shoulders. "I was a little surprised." She's surprised. I'm very surprised. I haven't thought about a girl in my house for almost three years now. My main focus in life was to find the truth out about my parents' death. Today is different. Since this morning when Gloria touched my arm and led me down the hall to wait on Gabriela, I have been wanting sex. Not just sex, I want to fuck someone hard. I almost screamed it at Gloria and Gabriela in the office but once they fired me, my urge went flying out the window. It wasn't until I got in my car and started driving, that the urge came back. I pulled up to a stoplight and a group of young college girls crossed in front of me. I thought I was going to blackout due to the lack of blood flow to my brain. The light turned green and I heard someone honking four times before I realized that they were honking at me. Seeing this girl standing right in front of me right now makes me feel bad though. I want her. I want her on top of me, screaming my name for hours. I know nothing about her though and I don't give a damn. I want her to be mine for the night and no one else.

My smile turns into a want more than a friendly hello and she sees the desire in her eyes.

"Bad day?" She takes my hand in hers and runs her finger up my arm until she reaches my neck. She is a few inches shorter than me, so she has to stand on her tippy toes as she slowly kisses my neck with her soft, tantalizing lips. "Let me take care of you."

My brain instantly goes back to the night I met Roxanna and I remember her taking charge and making me feel great. She didn't just make me feel great once, we fucked that night for hours. I take a deep breath in and smell this girl's coconut skin, as her tongue slides up my neck to my ear. I shiver all over as she teases me, making me want her more than ever. I think about grabbing her and taking her to my room for some relief, but I am enjoying this tease she is giving me. Gabriela pissed me off so much that I need to forget about her. I need to get her out of my head. If she doesn't want anything to do with me, then I don't want anything to do with her.

"What are you doing Dean?" I say under my breath. The girl stops kissing my neck and sinks back down onto her heels.

"Are you ok?" She asks sincerely. I don't know how to answer her. I want to say yes but I'm not ok. This is not ok. I don't even know what her name is or anything about this girl and I am about to take her inside and ravage her. For what? This makes no sense to me.

"I'm sorry," I say as pull her arm from my neck and kiss her hand softly. Her eyes are deep with hurt and pain but it's not from me. Something else is going on with her, just like there is something else going on with me. We both need each other today for some odd reason to take care of one another and I don't know what has drawn us so close to this moment in time, but we are.

"Relax." She whispers as her lips find mine. Strawberry lip gloss mixes with my lip and her tongue presses its way through to find mine. I let a soft moan as I reach in my pocket and pull out my key for the front door. Now my keyring is down to two keys, so finding the right one was easy and the door was open in a flash. Our lips never part as we make our way inside the small house and the smell of leftover pizza robs my nose of her sweet smell for a second.

"I'd love to have you wrapped around me as I fuck you hard." Where the hell did that come from? I don't normally talk like that but she has me memorized as we make our way to the bedroom, knocking over everything on our way.

She giggles and I think I catch her off guard because she stops kissing me and whispers in my ear. "Not yet." Before she can say anything else I grab her by the waist and pull her into the room.

"Oh!" She lets out a little moan as I start toward the bed with her. I kiss her neck and pull at her shirt. I stop kissing her neck for a second as I pull her shirt over her head and toss it in the corner. It slides down the wall and comes to stop on the carpet. She isn't wearing a bra and her breast fall back down after the force of the shirt being torn from her body.

I grab her breast in one hand and squeeze it as I start kissing down her neck to her chest. Her legs are wrapped around my waist and she's thrusting with her hips the more I kiss her. I suck in her sweet, soft nipple in my mouth as I lick the tip of it with my tongue.

"OH!" She screams while I have her breast in my mouth, enjoying the sweet taste of her skin, I have my hand sliding toward her shorts. I can feel her legs tighten as I get closer to her warm center.

"Not. Yet." She manages to get out as she pushes me down on the bed. I don't want to wait anymore and play any more games with her. I want to be inside her as she moans my name. She pulls my dress pants off me and I toss my shirt in the growing pile of clothes against the wall. She lowers herself down to her knees in front of me as I am waiting and ready for her next move.

I thought her tongue was great inside my mouth, but she is a goddess on her knees.

"You can't have all the fun," I demand as I toss her on the bed and plunge my fingers deeper into her and push her on the bed more, her legs are up and back against the bed, and she has her knees bent as I slid down off the bed to my knees. I kiss her inner thigh as I make my way to her wet, juicy center. I take my tongue and lick her up and down as she grasps my head and pulls my hair. I don't care what she does, I want to taste her. I normally don't like to do that to girls but I'm not thinking clearly tonight and I want everything. I need it. I need her all to myself. The more I lick the more she moves and moans louder. She starts begging and crying for me to be inside of her. She tastes like sweet honey as she becomes as wet as a river of honey in my mouth. YUM! She's perfect and she's what I need.

"Dean! Please. Please. I need you." She begs for me as our fire rages inside and grows with every touch. I can't take it anymore as I stand up and slowly enter her moist center. We cry out at the same time as I can't fight the feeling anymore.

"Awww! YES! YES! GOD! Don't stop!" She screams for more. Without mercy, I pound her as hard as I can to get the memory of Gabriela out of my head. I grab her hips and pull her in deeper toward my sweaty body until her body is covered with the aroma of both of us.

We both fall over on the bed and pass out from the heat of the hour.

Dean

Why can't I get her out of my head though? I've heard of love at first sight, but I don't believe that shit. But how else could I explain the feelings that I have for her? The stranger is still in my bed as morning comes and I kiss her forehead and then slide out of bed.

"WOW!" She laughs as she stretches from under the cover. "My last count was six. Is that accurate?"

I shake my head as I find some shorts to slide on for the day. "I'm sorry for last night. I don't normally act like that." I try to explain my actions, but she doesn't care.

"I loved it," she smiles biting her lip and giggling, "need me again, please call."

"Thanks, I had fun too." I pause for a minute because it just hit me that I don't know what her name is. We just had a full night of exciting and I have no clue who she is.

"Bethany, Bethany Brooks sweetheart." She giggles as she slides out of bed, dropping the blanket to the ground. She is very comfortable with her body and doesn't care to show it off.

Call it a distraction or call it a good time, but I needed

it last night. I walk Bethany out to her car and she drives off as the morning sun begins to rise. It's a cool morning but I know the heat will be setting in before too long, summer isn't over yet.

As Bethany drives away, a new Maserati, solid black with blacked-out windows eases into the drive. It becomes apparent pretty fast that this is someone with money that is parked in my drive.

"Wrong house," I yell as I start to walk up the porch to go inside. The driver's door opens, and I see long, tan legs stretch out of the car. High heels make contact with the ground and push the legs out. They seem to stretch forever and then are met by a tight black skirt. I can't see really well who it is that is getting out of the car, but I know they are beautiful.

"Dean," a voice calls out to me. "Dean, we need to talk."

It's Gabriela. Maybe I don't want to talk to her. Maybe I am happy with just parting ways and being done with her altogether. She was the reason for last night and she is to blame for me losing my job.

"What do you want?" I say in a mean tone. "Do you want to tell me I need to leave the city also?" I know I'm being an asshole and I don't give a shit right now. I don't know anything about her and I don't care about knowing anything about her.

"Dean, it's not safe for you here." She isn't making any sense. "We had a connection in the office and I can't just walk away from that, but-. But once I found out who you are. You just need to leave. Please, listen to me." She begins to say more and I stop her.

"What do you mean, you found out who I am?" I step down off the porch and stalk toward her. I don't know if I'm ready for a fight or to have a night like I just had with Bethany but with her. "I've found out a little of who you are on the internet. Your name is Gabriela Vaduva and you are a snake. You own three hospitals and now are in charge of the pharmaceutical. But other than that, I can't find much more about you."

"I guess you looked up what Vaduva means? Black widow. I live up to name in every aspect." Her phone rings and she has a troubled look on her face. "Hello," she says. I can't hear the other person on the line but I can tell by the sound in her voice something is wrong. "Fine," she screams to the other person. "Fuck you." She throws her phone in the car. "I told you, Dean. I can't be around you anymore, I've been told to stay away from you."

"What the hell are you talking about?" She isn't making sense. We met once and it wasn't that for that long and it was under the worse pretenses ever. She fired me and now she wants to come to my house and act like she has feelings for me?

I start to take a step toward her to see what her reaction will be. If she steps away, not wanting a physical touch, then maybe I'm not crazy in thinking we had a connection.

"Stop!" Her face turns white as she opens her door. "Don't make this harder than it already is."

Who had warned her? I want to ask her more questions, but she lowers herself into her car and leaves before I can. Why does everyone leave me? Why does this keep happening? I didn't understand what she is talking about. Gabriela knows me or says she knows me? I don't know how she is.

Nothing has ever worked out for me. My parents are dead and the one and the only person I could confide in left me, and now the job that could shed some light on what happened to them has slipped through my fingertips. That's it, I'm getting my job back. I'm changing the outcome this time around. I decide that I want to fight for my job and I'm going to do whatever it takes to get it back. I head to the ambulance service about midday the next morning, I figure everyone I need to talk to will be there then. When I pull in, I see the black Maserati in the parking lot.

"You can do this." I take a deep breath and try to

calm my nerves. I'm going to confront her about my job, and about who is threatening her. I want the truth, no matter what that is. If I find out we already know each other and there is more to her that I don't know yet, then so be it.

I get out of my car and start heading for the front doors. I can still see the women inside typing away but this time there is security walking around inside.

"Dean."

"Yes?" I turn to see a young blonde-haired girl getting out of her car. Looking at her body, she looks no more than nineteen, but seeing her face you'd swear she was a lot younger. She carries herself well and doesn't need an ounce of makeup for her perfect skin. She looks so innocent and sweet.

"What are you doing here? Everyone said you quit." Her blonde hair blows in the wind and I'm lost in her big blue eyes as she speaks.

"Um. No. I didn't quit." I say confused by her question and stunned by her beauty.

"I'm sorry, I'm Angelica." She can tell I have a confused look on my face and that I'm not sure who the hell she is. "You don't recognize my voice?" Again, I look at her with a confused look. I don't recognize her voice, but it's soft and sweet and very innocent. She sounds like an angel that has come to protect me from all evil. I've heard a voice close to that once, but the pain only comes to mind when I try to place it.

"I'm…" I'm not sure what I'm trying to get out but whatever it is, it's not coming. "Umm. I don't know who you are." I sheepishly say as she flashes a smile at me. "Should I know you?"

A long time ago I used to have a dream about a soft-spoken voice that would call to me. It would call my name and over time, the dreams became more and more vivid. One dream has always stuck out in my mind as I heard the voice calling my name.

"Dean. Dean." Over and over again it called. I followed the sound of her voice through the dark house until I reached the living room. Everything was pitch black, but the voice was clear as day. "Dean, Dean. I want you Dean." I found my way closer to the voice and I felt something grab my arm to pull me in closer. Soft lips touched my ear as it sang. "Dean. Oh, Dean. I want you. Give me that body." The warm breath was in my ear and my hair would stand up on my neck. Goosebumps rushed across my body as my pants became too tight. "Dean, Dean-." Behind my zipper was a large bulge, ready to spring out into the darkness. "Dean, Dean. Mmm-." The soft lips would find the tip of me and her tongue would pull at the rest of me as her lips earned for more. My name would still fill the air as muffled sounds now. "Dean, Dean."

I open my eyes, not realizing that I am not home dreaming anymore, and the sweet, soft voice is now an actual person and she is standing in front of me. "Shit!" I gasp as she stares a hole through my head.

"Shit?" She says as she puts her hands on her hips. "What does that supposed to mean?"

I'm searching for the words in my head but there isn't anything coming to mind. "Nothing," I say as I try to push my excited back down before she notices.

"Funny." She looks down at my hands and laughs even more. "All guys are the same."

"I…..." I don't know what I was planning on saying but I'm glad when she interrupts me.

"Where have you been if you didn't quit? I've been wanting to catch up with you." She smiles and looks at me with her deep blue's again. They're piecing and perfect.

"I, um. I was fired." I say while trying not to smile.

"So, it is true?" She stands straight up and puts her hands on her hips. "You are fucking that bitch, or did you just get excited when you first met her too? Pig!"

I look down at my pants and shake my head. What am I supposed to say to that? She has a point, I should just get in my car and leave. "Maybe. I don't know what happened." I shake my head and keep it down, hoping she will say something to make me feel better.

She snarls her nose at me and shakes her head. "Have you not heard the rumors sounding this chick? She's crazy. I mean psycho crazy."

"What do you mean?" It's odd the way she talks about Gabriela, almost like she knows more about her than the average person. Almost like they are related. I'm curious about what she's talking about.

"Let me put it like this, if she finds something she likes, she sinks her fangs into it and destroys it. Sometimes the men survive but others don't. She can break your whole world and have it come crashing down on you in no time. Trust me. I thought-. Never mind. Forget it." I'm dumbfounded by the way she talks about Gabriela. I search her face to see if she has witnessed this first hand or if she's just heard rumors. "So, are you here to beg for your job back?"

"I was planning on talking to her and seeing if I can work here again? I have been here for three years."

"Figures." She says with a disgusted look on her face. "If I were you, I'd run, and stay far away from that crazy chick. She won't be able to leave you alone now. She fired you to just play with you. She normally will pick a few employees from each new place she owns and does the same thing to them. They always come running back."

"I don't understand. You work here?" I say, a matter of fact.

"I didn't have a choice. But you. You're going to ask her for your job back and then she will want to see you after work and that will turn into more. You're a fool. You're just like all the other idiots that get bit by her. Wake up and start thinking with your real head and not your dick for once." Her words sting as they hit me like a ton of bricks. "I'm late for work." She turns and heads toward the door shaking her head. Before she opens it, she turns and smiles at me. "Good luck. I hope to see you again though. I have missed you, a lot." I grin at her, but I don't remember ever meeting her. "I've really missed seeing you. It's been way too long." She says as the door closes behind her.

It's been too long? What's that supposed to mean? I walk into the main office and head straight for Gabriela's office with security behind me, trying to stop me from barging in.

When I get to her door security grabs my arms and starts to pull me back away from it.

"Let him go." She says as security lets go of me. "Come on in Dean. Sit down." My hands begin to shake as I wasn't expecting to make it this far. What do I do now? Angelica had opened my eyes in the parking lot and made me think twice about even coming in to ask for my job back. "So, I guess you want your old job back?" How did she know? Did someone tell her?

I take a seat and wait for her to make the first move. I don't know why I feel powerless around her but I'm afraid for some odd reason. I look up from my chair to see long tanned legs crossed in front of me as she sits on the edge of her desk with a pencil skirt and top that makes her breast pop out when she leans forward. My mind is everywhere but where it needs to be right now and I'm not sure if this is a dream or what.

"Gabriela," I swallow hard, "I would like to know if I could continue to work here?" That wasn't that bad. I did it. I asked. *Now what?*

"Honey!" She says as she leans forward, giving me a glance down her shirt. "If you really want to continue to work here then that's fine. I think we can accommodate." She stands up and walks around her desk slowly, making her heels click with every seductive step she takes. "But you better be careful, I have heard that there is an employee that has taken an interest in you. You know the rules here, no dating among employees." What? Angelica? She said hi to me. I just met her today and now there is a rumor about us? Before I can form a sentence she smiles and leans over her desk toward me. This time her round breast spills out of her lace bra as the shirt opens up. She knows she's hot and she is trying to distract me. I try to look away but my head and eyes won't let me. I hear Angelica's voice in my head warning me of Gabriela. Warning me to stay away.

"I don't plan on dating anyone, from work," I say through gridded teeth, trying to make sure that she knows I'm talking mainly about her.

"Good, 'cause I hate to fire a great employee for crossing the line." She's laying her accent on thick as she speaks. The more she gets worked up, the more it comes out.

"Wait! What?" I try to correct her and tell her nothing is going on between me and Angelica but she stops me mid-sentence.

"Just do what you're told and nothing else. And keep your mouth shut." She points out the door and I take my queue to walk out.

Have I put Angelica's job in jeopardy by talking with her this morning? What has happened here? Was she watching us this morning? I want to ask more questions but Gabriela isn't in the mood of answering anything else. As soon as I step out of her office she slams the door and I go to the supervisor to get my new schedule.

I went straight back to work and was ready for it also. Nothing had changed downstairs and I don't think anyone knew I was gone. I love working by myself and this job let me be all by myself.

The day seems to go about the same as every day before I was fired, but now I am looking harder for answers about my parents. I know I need access to the archive room but I'm not sure how to get in there.

"I see she is giving you another chance." Angelica comes out of nowhere and scares the shit out of me. She has a grin on her face. "Did you have to sell your soul to her?"

I laugh at first, but then start wondering if I did.

"I, don't think so." I try to laugh but I'm not sure. "I know she doesn't like you very much." Why did I just say that? Seriously.

"I know." Angelica grins and leans in close to my ear. "I don't like her either." Now I laugh, maybe more than I should have. Some employees at the other end of the hall turn around and snarl at us.

"Have a great day." I say as I open the door to my room.

"You too." I don't know why Gabriela doesn't like Angelica. She's so nice and sweet and I don't think she has a mean bone in her toned, little perfect body. I step back out in the hall for a second to see where she works at. "Archives? No way?"

The rest of the day I try to think of a way to ask Angelica if she would let me into the archive room. Maybe I should just tell her why I want in there and she would understand. She might understand. I don't know. I play it over and over again in my head and when I finally get enough nerve up to go ask her, I realize it's time to clock out and go home.

As I walk to my car I notice that my gas cap is open. "Did someone steal my gas?"

I walk slowly to see if anyone is around the car still, but the parking lot is empty.

"Dean, wait up." Angelica's sweet voice calls out. I turn to look at her, thinking this will be as good of a time as any to talk to her about the archive room.

I hear a sizzling sound coming from my car behind me. Angelica is a few yards away and I turn to look at the car to see what is making the noise. The sound stops suddenly as I turn back around to Angelica, smiling, ready to talk with her.

"Dean!" She yells as I am thrown forward by an

explosion that deafens me. My back is hit with flying debris as my car is torn apart in seconds. I am tossed like a rag doll, ten feet or more before I land face-first on the blacktop in front of Angelica.

Dean

"Lorenzo? Have you heard anything from Roxanna? I've tried calling her a few times and I haven't been able to get in touch with her." Lorenzo owns a club downtown that heard Roxanna was working at before. I don't know if she is still working there or what she is doing anymore but I would love to see her again.

"Dean, forget her. Just forget her." He didn't act like his scumbag self like he normally does. He's mellow and sincere.

"I can't. I know all we had fun and stuff, but I can't just forget her. I can't just act like there was nothing there." Why can't he see how great she is? Even though Roxanna is a stripper and possibly a prostitute, I still feel a connection to her in some weird way. Maybe it was because she took my virginity but I still want to make sure is ok.

"Dean, she's gone. She burned her bridges and she isn't coming back. So drop it." Lorenzo is back to his scumbag self now.

I slowly start to wake up and hold my head as I try sitting up. I don't know why memories of Roxanna keep popping in my head, but they have more and more in the past few weeks.

"Dean, this is Detective Moore. He has some

questions for you." I'm still dazed as I sit on the
ground for a little while, waiting for my head to stop
spinning. I didn't notice Angelica talking to anyone
next to me, but when I looked up, I see a small guy in
height, but with a large frame, and strong chin, in a
nice suit standing next to me. He has his badge
hanging from his neck and a Sig P226 on his right
side. A very expensive gun, even for a Detective. His
hair is short brown and I can see a 5 o'clock shadow
starting to show on his face. He has some cuts above
his right eye and what looks like a tattoo on his neck
going down to his back. It looks like he's fit and that
he knows how to fight, the bruising on his knuckles
and the swollen lip makes it clear of that. "He's an
old friend, Dean."

Detective Moore, or old friend, as Angelica called
him, is asking every question he could think of. Most
of the questions are straightforward, how long I've
been working here and if someone had a beef with me
and why I thought someone wanted to kill me or hurt
me.

"So, Dean, you're telling me that you just started back
to work today after being let go a couple weeks ago?"
He's writing in a book as he asks his questions.

"That's right. Just started back today. I'm not sure
why I was let go in the first place, something stupid I
guess but it was overturned and now I'm back." I

didn't want my whole life story laid out for this guy to know.

"What were you fired for?"   He stops writing and looks at me while I try to think of a good reason I was fired.

"Um. Well, I was." I pause and try to find the right words to say.

"Gabriela." Angelica chimes in.

"Thanks a lot, Angelica. Damn." I glare at her. Everyone standing around start shaking their heads as they understand what happened to me.

"I see, so you were fucking her and she fired you after she had her fun or what?" Detective Moore never stops writing as he turns to look at Angelica that has her arms crossed. She is giving him a sideways glare that would make me run and hide but he just laughs at her. "Ok, so you weren't fucking her?" He shakes his head and rolls his shoulders up to ask her if that's right. She nods in approval. "Have you noticed anyone strange around here or know why someone would want your friend dead Angelica?"

Friend? We just meet the other day. Are we friends?

"I know that Gabriela has had some run-ins with some of her other." She pauses for a minute and looks around. "Men."

"Thanks, Angelica, for sharing your thoughts of me."
Gabriela walks up behind where we are sitting.
"Detective, I can't think of anyone that would want to
hurt any of my employees. As for our relationship, as
you so delicately put it, I haven't had the pleasure
yet." My mind races as I try to make sense of what
she just said, I haven't had the pleasure yet. What the
hell is she talking about?

"If any of you think of anything, call me or the office
and let us know. We don't have much to go on here."
The Detective turns and walks away after he gives
Angelica a half hug.

What am I going to do? My car is gone, destroyed
and I have no way home. I loved my car, it was the
one memory of my mom that I have wanted to keep
all these years. Why did it have to be my car? Of all
things.

"Dean," the sweet voice of Angelica breaks into my
thoughts.

"Sorry, did you say something?" I wasn't listening to
her as she lowers herself down on the ground next to
me. The only thought going through my mind right
now is my car. "I said, do you need me to take you
home?" She looks worried and points toward her car.

"I can't ask you to do that." I need a ride home, but I
don't want her wrapped up in my mess. I would love

60

to ask her about the archive room but I don't think now would be the best time to ask her.

"Come on." She pulls me to my feet and starts walking to her car and doesn't look back. I follow because I need a ride home.

"What about Gabriela, she warned me to stay away from you or she would fire you." I say as I hold my aching head.

"Don't worry about her. She can't touch me. Trust me." I don't argue with her, mainly because I want to be around her more.

We don't talk much in the car and she drives slow for being a teenager. When we pull up to my house she has a troubled look on her face.

I can't take it any longer. "What?" I have to know what she's thinking. Her blonde hair is pulled back in a ponytail and I can see that she's a natural blonde and her skin is silky smooth. She isn't wearing makeup and there is no reason for her to. She is an angel sent from heaven.

"You don't remember do you?" I'm dumbfounded by the question as I stare at her face and try to tell if she is joking or not. I shake my head. "Fine." She shakes her head in disbelief. "When you do remember, if you ever do, let me know. Also, stay away from Gabriela. I'm telling you, she's dangerous."

"Um, ok." I say as I slowly exit her car. "Thank you."

"You're welcome, Dean. You've always been really sweet." I close the door still not knowing what she is talking about. She thinks that I know her, but I don't remember her. As she drives off and I slap myself.

"I forgot to ask her about the archive room." Too late now Dean, you idiot. I walk into the house for some much-needed rest.

The night went by way to fast and I was not ready for the alarm clock to go this morning. I get up and brush my teeth and find something to wear for the day. My keys to the car are normally laying in a bowl next to the door but this time when I reach in, all I find is one key left on the key ring.

"Oh yeah, my car exploded." I chuckle a little as I look down at my keys. I used to have three keys on the ring but now I have only one left. Work never gave me my key back but everything has changed so much at work I don't think they will ever use keys again.
I walk outside and Angelica is sitting in the drive waiting on me.

"You work this weekend?" Angelica asks as I slide into the passenger seat.

"Not sure yet. I need to go in and check on something but not sure if I can." I buckle up and wait for Angelica to back out of the drive.

"Do you need a ride?" She smiles as she puts the car in reverse and backs out.

"Are you working this weekend?" I want to ask her about the archive room but I'm afraid of asking her since she says she knows me somewhere.

"If you need something just ask me. Geez, you love to beat around the bush don't you."

We pull into work and I hoop out of the car, ready to start this day. Angelica steps out and I realize she's shorter than I am and if I lean forward my chin would rest on her head. Her hair glows as the sunlight hits it and her eyes are as blue as the ocean. I don't see a wrinkle one on her young face.

"Do you work in the records room?" I finally just blurt it out before it eats me alive.

"Yes." She is hesitant on answering me but she does with a slow yes, unsure of where I am going with the question.

"I want to know what happened to my mom and dad.

You see, they died many years ago and they worked for this company." I want to tell her more but she cuts me off.

"Oh, I see. Well. See you around, Dean." She quickly turns and walks inside the building without saying another word.

"Son of Bitch!" I scream once the door closes behind her. How can I be so fucking stupid? I knew I shouldn't have asked her. She probably only thinks I've been nice to her so I could use her.

The rest of the day I can't stop thinking of Angelica's face and the way it made me feel inside. I work fast and keep busy just so I don't have to talk to anyone else. When lunchtime came, I ate by myself and then went for a run around the block to clear my mind.

Angelica text me earlier and said that she would take me home if I needed her to. I'm glad too, I want to explain more of why I need to look in the archive room. I told her that she doesn't have to, but she said it's no big deal. I thought I might have scared her off this morning, but she had to text me and said she doesn't mind taking me. We have around ten minutes before we both get off and I'm watching the clock like a hawk.

"Dean, my office, now!" Shit, it's Gabriela. It's been nice to avoid her for a while but I knew this day was coming eventually.

I walk into Gabriela's office and she's perched on the edge of her desk in a small mini skirt that starts halfway up her knee. I study her legs for a minute and realize I'm staring at her body with more intent than I aim to. My eyes make their way up to her stomach and it is flat with some of her skin showing from where her top doesn't come down far enough. I can make out the belly ring and the hint of a tattoo that I remember seeing the other day. Her hair is pulled back in a bun but it's as dark as the night sky. Her lips are bright red and she makes sure to bite the lower lip when she sees me looking at her. Her eyes are dark all around them and her pupils cut through me like a knife.

"Can I help you?" I swallow hard trying not to get excited as the goddess teases me with her smile. She makes me want to take her where she stands. What's wrong with me?

"I want to see if you have plans for dinner?" WHAT? She has blown me off this long and now she wants to have dinner. What's wrong with this chick?

"I had planned on going home and doing nothing." I try to sound like that's the only thing I want to do, but dinner does sound good. Not to mention she's rich, so it would be something good.

"Just go to dinner with me and we can talk. I would love to get to know you some." ***BULLSHIT***. She's up to something I know it. She pushes off her desk and starts my way like a lioness on the hunt. Her eyes are locked on her pray as she lines up for her kill. "It'll be my treat." Her fingers brush my face as she walks by me. I turn to see her ass bounce as her heels click toward the door.

I never answer her but I follow her out the door toward the parking lot. Most everyone has left for the day as I follow Gabriela out to her car. Angelica is leaning on her car, waiting for me as I walk past her, in a trance by Gabriela's poison.

"He's mine tonight." The words sound hateful as Gabriela shoots an evil glare toward Angelica. Her face sinks with dismay as I continue to walk mesmerized behind Gabriela. I hear a huff come from behind me and I turn to see a disgusted look on Angelica's face as her door slams shut.

"Angelica." I try to cry out but it's too late. Smoke fills the air as she speeds off.

"Good, she's out of the way." A smirk comes from Gabriela's face. Was this her evil plan from the beginning? Did she just do this to hurt Angelica? But why? Why does she want to hurt the sweetest girl alive? Angelica would give you her last breath to a complete stranger and not think twice about it.

"You did this on purpose?" I know the evil conniving bitch tricked me and I played right into her game. What was I was thinking?

"Dean, no." Her tone changes and her expression go soft. She runs to me, throwing herself in my arms. "I need you, Dean. I need you inside me again. I need to feel every each of your body inside my aching body." Gabriela weeps for me and it feels nice for some reason. For the first time in a long while, I feel needed. "I love you, Dean." She buries her face in my chest and weeps for me more. What's going on with her? Last week she didn't want anything to do with me and this week, she loves me? I stand dumbfounded as I hold her in my arms.

Dean

Angelica hasn't returned any of my calls and she
won't talk to me at work anymore. Gabriela and I
never made it to dinner the other night like she said
she wanted to. She stayed in my arms for a few
minutes and then said she would drive me home.
When we reached the house she didn't waste any time
making sure I was ready for her. The lock on the door
couldn't have been unlocked any faster as we ran into
the house. Before she even stepped through the door,
her top was off and she was shimming out of her skirt.
I really wanted to watch the show but she had pushed
me down to the couch and told me to shut up. I don't
know if it was the rush of the moment or the power
she displayed, but I was more than ready for her. She
didn't waste any time as she lowered herself on the
floor in front of me and pulled my manhood out. I
didn't need any warm-up for her but she still gave me
a few strokes before she swallowed me whole. I cried
out as she worked me up and down, never stopping to
a breath as her head bobbed up and down. I wanted to
do so much to her but every time I would try to stand
up, she would push me back down the couch. I was
hers and she was getting what she wanted from me.
As I drew nearer to my end, she sensed the tightening
and worked harder. She was controlling me and I
could do nothing but enjoy the moment. At least I
could not hold my excitement back anymore as she

took me deep in her mouth. She only gasped a little as boiled over and exploded like a volcano of passion. My night was far from being over as she pulled me to the bedroom. Passion and lust would not compare to the night that we shared. The next morning she was gone without a kiss goodbye or even a hug.

A few days went by and Angelica had stopped giving me rides to and from work altogether. I ended up breaking down and buying a car, a cheap one for now, just in case someone wanted to blow this one up also. I need something to get me back and forth to work for now. Gabriela keeps teasing me as she sinks her teeth deeper into me. I let it get out of hand from time to time and I don't know why I can't resist her. I get flustered when she starts her games with me at work but I try to be as strong as I can. I get worked up and I have thoughts of taking her on her desk and don't care who might see us. I'm able to control myself and I know I need to stay away from her. Gabriela seems to only start making big moves on me in the hallway at work when Angelica is near. She thinks this is a game and loves it when she is caught flirting with me. I try to resist the urge that I have but she smells amazing. Gabriela starts kissing my neck as Angelica walks up behind her. Knowing that Angelica is watching makes her go more on the *slut* attack. She pulls at my ear lobe with her teeth as she whispers dirty things in my ear as she pushes me against the wall. I am powerless to her temptations and want to relive the night we shared together. She's showing the innocent girl that she's the top predator around and not to think about taking her meal. Why am I caught in the middle of this war? A war between two women that are in different classes. Gabriela is experienced and she knows how to twist and turn to make the Pope himself think of sinning for a night. Angelica is a good girl with a body that most women kill for or try to buy but hers is natural.

"Get a room." Angelica snarls as she passes.

"I'm sorry princesses, am I making you uncomfortable?" Gabriela's words mock Angelica. She knows that she can have any guy that she wants and there's nothing Angelica can do to stop her. Seeing Angelica makes me snap out of the daze that Gabriela has me in.

"Angelica, wait." I push past Gabriela to catch Angelica by the arm. "Please, talk to me." It's been too long since the last time I heard her sweet voice. She's been avoiding me but I want to talk to her and get to know her. I know we are connected somehow but Angelica won't give me the time of day to try and find out how.

"You looked like you were enjoying the sluts tongue too much to talk." Angelica's teeth grind in her mouth as her eyes turn from blue to red. She hates

70

Gabriela with more than just a passion, but why? Did she hate her because of me? Or is there more of their past that I don't know yet?

"Can we talk?" I press as her hateful eyes turn to me and a grin comes across her face.

"You made your bed, now go sleep in it." She turns and stalks off down the hall.

"That girl never could take any competition," Gabriela says as she turns and walks back to her office like nothing happened.

"Is this a fucking game to you?" I blurt out as employees are moving from room to room.

"The sooner you figure out it's a game for one of them and not the other, you'll be a better man." An elderly man slaps me on the back and turns to walk off. "It's always been a competition between those two. You're going to have to choose at some point."

What did he mean, it has always been a competition? I thought Angelica was a good girl and Gabriela was the slut? Do they lure men in for fun and see who can get them first?

 The next few shifts of working with Gabriela and Angelica is starting to get to be too much for me. Angelica still won't talk to me and Gabriela wants in my pants, only when Angelica is around. Gabriela calls me into her office wearing shorter and shorter skirts each day, just making sure I can see everything she has. She makes sure to only call me in when Angelica sees us together. When I leave, she presses against me and tells me how good I was, even though I was in her office for run reports and time card issues. She's playing a game and I keep falling for it time and time again. The more she does, the more I want her though. I want to walk into her office and bend her over her desk, push her skirt up and pound her while she screams my name so everyone in the building can hear her. I can't stop thinking about it. I dream about her at night, over and over again. I still dream of Angelica and her sweet voice as well. I am torn inside and I am about to lose control.

"Dean, Gabriela needs you in the office. Again." One of the office ladies tells me when I'm leaving for the day. It's starting to be an everyday thing now with her. She wants to make sure Angelica sees me walking into her office when she leaves for the day.

"Dean, come in." Gabriela says as I knock on the half-closed door to her office. "Have a seat, I have a question for you." She is wearing the shortest skirt I've ever seen in my life. Dark green and tight, with a little blouse on that cuts very low in the front. She isn't wearing a bra and her fake breast are bouncing with every movement she makes. Her nipples are showing through the shirt like it's zero degrees outside and sweat starts to form on the back of my neck as I try not to stare at her. She steps to the edge of the desk, pushing her tight little ass up on the edge of it. Stretching her long, tanned legs out and crossing them at the ankles. My eyes go from her lips, where she sucks in her bottom lip, biting it with a grin. Falling down to her neck and then to her blouse that is over her cleavage that's showing entirely too much of her. Even though she leaves little to the imagination, I do imagine them in my mouth. This is torture and should be illegal. Seeing her big breast with her hard nipples poking out at me as me readjust what's making my pants tighter. My eyes follow on down her body, past her flat stomach to her short skirt. She has it pulled up high for me where it is sowing the bottom of her cheeks. Her long, tanned legs are stretched out with her ankles crossed. Her high heels are flicking up and down like a snake, mesmerizing her prey with every movement. My eyes go up and down with every motion of her heel as she controls my body once again. She isn't the snake though as she moves up and down. She is the one playing the music, mesmerizing me while she plans out her next move.

"Dean, you are going to dinner with me tonight." She doesn't ask me to dinner or even invites me to join her. She demands that I go with her and I am powerless to disagree with her. I agree to whatever she wants. "Good." She pushes herself off the desk and walks back to her chair. I am still lost for words as I see her intertwine her feet as she does her runway walk around the desk. My eyes go back and forth as I watch her skirt move from side to side. My only thought is that I wish I was buried deep inside her.

The rest of the day is a blur and I manage to get out of her office before acting on my thoughts with her. I don't remember driving home and once there I get ready for my date tonight. She didn't give me any idea of where we were going or what to wear for our date, so I put on the best clothes I had and waited for her. A stretch limo pulls up to the house late in the evening and waits for me to make my way to it.

"Hi, sexy." Gabriela is in a short skirt, again. They are her favorite things to wear around me because she knows it turns me on to no end. The skirt shows everything you want to see when she sits down she makes sure to cross her legs slowly so I can enjoy the view. She's wearing a top that is two sizes too small in the chest and she is about to pop a seam, revealing her perky breast.

"Hi." I can't think of anything else to say because she has me lost for words. What am I doing? I know that if I get in that limo with her, I would end up inside her. Somehow, I managed to get out of her office today without taking her, but I don't see how I can make it through the night without repeating the other night with her.

I step to the limo wearing black dress slacks and a blue button-up silk shirt. Guys that are fit look dumb in dress clothes and everything is too tight for me to wear but I know most women like a guy dressed up. If I start to get excited tonight, everyone will see pretty quickly.

Mmm, god, she smells good. She has a way to poison me, but I don't give a damn right now. Her hair is up on top of her head with a few curls coming down one side.

"I want my hands in your hair as I fuck your ass on the way to dinner."

"So, you approve? I won't stop you if you think you are man enough, I'll enjoy every throbbing inch of it." Damn, did I just say that out loud? Approve? Hell no, I want. I want to dive into her wet center and stay all night. My brain stops thinking due to blood loss and I am frozen outside of the limo as I dream of her bending over. I can feel my bulge getting bigger and bigger and I know my pants don't have room for me to grow anymore. I take a deep breath before I explode with excitement.

"Come on in here. I won't bite. Too hard, unless you want me to." Her grin is devilish as she throws her head back at her own joke. I try to turn and run but my legs won't move. I know better than to get in the limo with her and I know where it will end up if do. If I fight this urge anymore, I will end up in the shower for hours tonight. I might as well get in the limo and see how much teasing she has in store for me.

"Where are we going?" I try to sound like I'm not interested in her and that this doesn't mean anything to me, but she's already heard me say I want her. She knows I belong to her tonight and she can have me anytime she wants.

"There's a little restaurant down the street. I know the owner." I lower myself into the limo and stay on the other side, away from her. I can't take my eyes off her as I watch her lick her lips and twirl what hair hanging down. She knows how to drive me crazy and she is doing a fine job at it. I finally can't take any more of it and step forward toward her side. I wrap my arm around her slender waist and pin her backward in the seat. I want her now and I plan on taking charge of her this time. As I slowly kiss her neck and press my waist into hers I am able to feel her warm under me. She is not resisting as I slide her skirt up higher so I drive deeper between her. As my hand slides down to unzip the limo turns into a parking lot full of expensive cars and people in suits walking in and out of a dimly lit building.

"So close Dean, you should have started earlier. We are here now. Have you ever been here before?" Gabriela smooths her skirt back down after she slides out from under me and steps out of the limo. I can see that she isn't wearing panties and her pink lips are swollen from our little encounter moments ago. She looks so wet and mouthwatering I already know what I want to order to eat. It's going to be a long night and she isn't going to make it easy for me.

"Ah. NO." I answer after my blood goes back to the rest of my body. I re-tuck my shirt and follow her to the front doors.

"Good." She says as she smiles and pulls my arm around her as we walk into the restaurant.

Angelica

I'm doing better about not thinking of Dean all the time. For the most part, I am able to avoid him at work but Gabriela has to rub my nose in the fact that she can take anything she wants. She knows that I can't stop her either. It's always been like this and it will always be like it. I hate her and she hates me so there is no love loss there. Gabriela is ten years older than I am and by far more experienced when it comes to men. She has the ability to have anyone she wants, and I've never had a man look at me twice, except for Dean. I'm nineteen and still a virgin and will be one for a long time to come. It's pathetic but I don't mind not knowing that part of life. I've had one boyfriend, if I can even call him that, for a few years. He took care of me when my mom died and then I started dating him. We both decided it was better if we remained friends and forgot that he had feelings for me. I guess I'm still too young for any type of relationship that is that intense. I miss my mom too much to try to love anyone right now. I think of her every day and I know she would want me to be happy. I need to forget Dean and forget Gabriela altogether. She's nothing but poison and she's going to kill someone with her poison one day.

I started working at my dad's restaurant downtown. He wants me to take over some of his businesses and start making, as he calls it, real money for myself. It isn't a bad job and I really like all the staff here. The girls that work here want to hit on all the old men as they try to make more money in tips, and they will tip. The waiters are all gay and try to be eye candy for the old women. It gets funny watching the old women stare at the waiter's butts as they walk by. But once another cute guy walks in, the waiters are staring at their butt. They really want to land an old rich man, but I've heard some of them say an old lady that's loaded would be nice too. Just as long as they didn't have to do anything with them. It's funny to see both compete to see who can make more money by the end of the night.

"Angelica, this is our new employee." One of the waiters comes up introducing a new server girl. She looks to be about my age with long blonde hair pulled up in a bun to keep it out of her face. We make the girls were short shorts with low cut shirts. All clothing is dark and my dad likes for the shirts to be too small for the girls. He loves to see as much skin as possible. Probably one reason he left my mom, she hated wearing anything revealing. The thought is, the more boobs that pop out in front of the old men, the more money they'll dish out. The guys must wear tight pants or shorts with a tight shirt. Also, dark colors. Nothing's supposed to be left to the imagination but keep the restaurant in a classy standard for the part of town it's in. He wants the guest to mentally have sex with their servers while they eat.

"I'm Angelica Muller. My dad is Nicholas Muller; he owns the restaurant and some other places around town. I expect all employees to conduct themselves with respect here and to flirt all they want with the customers. But, nothing else. At least not at work. What you do in your free time is your business." I try to smile and sound light-hearted as I hate that speech. I've heard my dad give it more times than I count to his new employees and I think it's a crop. Of course, he doesn't mind if a server girl goes into his office to have fun with him while on the job. Dad told me that when you get caught up with a customer, it never turns out good, for anyone. But I guess to him, the boss is always fair game.

"Thank you, I'll try and not let you down." The blonde is a cutie with nice features. She is filled out more than me and by her grins and biting her lip every now and then, I would say she is more experienced than I. Her makeup is applied thick and she has a skinny waist and big breasts. She'll do fine.

Dean

"I don't think I have ever heard of this place before," I tell Gabriela as we walk into a large room filled with old men and women. There's marble flooring throughout the dining room with large chandeliers hanging from the ceiling. There are what looks like real diamonds hanging from each of them. Each table has four different forks and more plates than what's in my apartment. "This is odd." I say as I take in all my surroundings. I can't get over how extravagant everything is.

"The food is great here, you will love it." Gabriela walks in looking like she owns the place. She wants the best table and expects everyone to fall to her feet as she walks.

"Ms. Vaduva right this way. Your table is ready." The hostess takes us to our table that's in the center of the room. It has the best view of the room and all its wonders.

"I'm going to get a drink." I turn to walk away from Gabriela toward the bar, I need to walk away for a minute and get my brain to start working.

"Don't get lost." She smiles as I'm walking off.

"Dean," a young blonde yells as she runs up to me, wrapping her arms around my neck.

"Bethany?" I never knew where she worked at and I never called her after our night of full passion and fun. She's wearing short shorts and a dark shirt that's two sizes too small and she looks smoking hot.

"How are you?" She stops midsentence and presses her hand to her mouth. "Are you on a date?" She grins big and lets out a giggle.

"No, I'm here with a friend." I try to convince myself that this is not a date but I don't think it's working.

"Oh, I see." She giggles. "Thought you were going to be with me forever. I thought we were soul mates after that night." She says as she bumps me. Laughing at her own words.

"What do you mean? After what night?" Gabriela snarls as she steps up behind both of us with her arms crossed. Shit! When did she leave the table?

"Nothing, Bethany is a friend I know." I say as quickly as I can. I don't know why I care if Gabriela knows that Bethany and I hooked up one night but it's none of her business.

"Whatever. You're a fucking liar. She's a fucking slut that wants to have someone in a better fucking class than her. She's nothing but fucking trash." Gabriela has fire in her eyes as she stares down at Bethany. She's on a warpath and poor Bethany is in her sights. I try to think of something fast to calm her down before she makes an even bigger scene the more she looks at her. Bethany's eyes began to fill with tears as Gabriela continues to insult her.

"Calm down Gabriela, Bethany is a sweet girl that I know." I did have sex with her one night and we had an amazing night of passion. She left and I never called or talked to her afterward but we had a connection for that moment in time. She was someone that I needed when I was depressed. Now Gabriela is attacking her, but why? We aren't dating or anything. This is the first time that I agreed to go out with her.

"Don't take up for this fucking slut." Gabriela barks as Bethany steps behind me for cover. She's ready for a fight and doesn't care where she is when she starts it.

Angelica

I hear people yelling on the floor and I'm trying to get to the noise before it gets any louder.

"What is your fucking deal? Just calm down and let's eat." I hear a male's voice speaking, trying to keep calm whoever he's with. The voice sounds familiar and I know I have heard that voice before, it sounds so familiar. Then I see him. Wearing tight slacks and an oh-so-tight button-up and down shirt. God, he looks sexy. I've tried so hard not to be attracted to him but seeing him today I know I'm doomed. I've seen him at work many times since we stopped talking but never like this. Work clothes don't make anyone look sexy but what he's wearing now makes my legs numb. I'm getting a warm sensation throughout my body that I've never had before. Why did I stop talking to this god? I think as I admire how perfect he is in every way. I didn't even know I wanted him, but I want him now. I need to quit staring and try to make everyone stop screaming before other people get up and leave. But I want to keep the vision of him taking his clothes off a little longer in my mind. Why did I leave him? Why?

"You stupid, white trash, fucking bitch." Oh, now I remember why I left him alone. Gabriela is having one of her, I'm mighty than tho, bitch fest and she is screaming at Bethany.

"Calm down. Damn. She was just saying hi."
Dean's still taking up for Bethany as she is hiding
behind his strong shoulders. I've never seen him take
up for anyone before. Normally when Gabriela's
around, he's consumed with her poison and can't take
his mind off her. What did Bethany mean to him?
Does he know her somehow? Is she another girl that
is caught up in his twisted game?

"What is your fucking deal Ms. High and Mighty?"
Bethany's starting to get brave as she is hiding from
Gabriela still.

"Bethany, that's enough!" I scream as I make my
way to where they are standing. "Go to the kitchen
and I'll be there in a minute." I try to sound like I'm
authoritative, but it's hard when I'm around Gabriela.
She knows me better than anyone and she knows that
I'm anything but authoritative. I need to get Bethany
away from her and Dean though before I have to fire
her on the spot.

"Angelica?" Dean looks stunned as he looks me up
and down. My long blonde hair is pulled up and I
have no makeup on at all. I'm wearing a tight shirt,
but I don't have boobs like Bethany or Gabriela, but
at least mine are real. He looks down at my waist and
I want to turn and run. I'm not fit and toned like the
other two women standing next to me and I'm not
wearing anything as revealing as them either. I

decided to wear shorts today but they are longer and not cut to my cheeks like the waitress's wear. He keeps my gaze for what seems like years. I want to ask him why he's staring at me so hard because I'm not a looker like any of the other women around. I'm plain and simple, but to him, I seem like the only girl in the room. He is taking me in for the first time as his eyes grow larger with love. I notice his blue eyes are a deep blue and they look like they have seen years of pain. They've always looked cold before but the way he is looking at me now they are coming to life. I wish I knew if he was thinking of me the same way I am thinking of him.

"What are you doing here? Where's Nicholas?" Gabriela's voice brings me back from my fantasy to face the fact that he's here with her. How could he? I want to grab the closest steak knife and jab it into his chest. I want him to feel the pain that I'm feeling right now as my heart is bursting open. I know I haven't talked to him in weeks, but how could he choose her?

"I am running the restaurant today?" I take a step closer to them both. "Is there something that I can help you with?"

"For starters, keep your slut waitresses off my date." Date? Is he really on a date with, *Black Widow*? She's nothing but poison and I don't know he can't see that.

"Wow, date?" Dean stops Gabriela from saying any more. "This was dinner, that's it." Is he trying to downplay their date for me or is he telling the truth? He looks worried about what she just said though. Is he here on a date with her, hoping to get laid? Or is he just having dinner with his boss?

"I'm sorry if one of my new girls stepped out of line and flirted a little too much with your, *date*." I make sure to emphasize, *date* when I say it. "I will have a talk with her about the rules for the restaurant." I turn to Dean to see the confusion on his face. The word, *date,* has thrown him for a loop. "Is there anything else I can help you with?" I want both of them to leave and I don't want them causing a scene on my first day of being boss. If dad finds out, he'll think I can't do this and he won't let me take over any of his businesses. Dad said I must prove to him I'm worthy to be my own boss. I told him I want to do what made me happy. I wanted to learn more of what my mom did but it came with a big catch from him. Gabriela would be my boss. I tried arguing with him and telling him that I could work somewhere else. He knows that I don't like her, but he thought we could be friends one day.

"I think we are good." Dean says as he shoots me a little grin. "Some people are just a little jealous." Oh, shit, Dean. Don't egg her on. Just let her be. I know he's trying to be funny and he's winking at me when he said it, but geez.

"I'm not jealous of some white trash, blonde bimbo, slut, that is working as a waitress to make ends meet." I think Dean is telling the truth about this not being a date because he just set Gabriela off. At least this time she's not dropping the F-bomb every other word but she is still fired up. Her face is red and she has hate in her eyes as she stares at Dean. Dad will surely tell me to find something else to do after she calls him. If I can't handle one small problem, then how would I handle anything else?

"Not jealous? Really? What do you call this?" Dean laughs and I can't help but think he's gone crazy. What is he doing? Gabriela is crazy and she will raise all kinds of hell until she gets her way. "If you're not jealous then you won't mind if I eat with Angelica and find out when she started running this great restaurant. I'm curious." Dean turns and smiles at me as he motions for me to join him.

What just happened? Did Dean just dump Gabriela to eat with me? No one has ever done that. Normally when we are in the same room together all eyes are on her and no one ever sees me.

"Um, well. I'm really busy." I try to sound like I'm working hard, but I want to spend time with him too.

I've missed him. I've never seen this side of him before and he is being so nice. It doesn't hurt either that he looks like a god right now.

"She said no. There, you happy. Now get your ass back over with me and eat like you said you would." Gabriela's getting her claws out now and I think she is madder now than she was earlier.

"If you wouldn't care, Angelica. My appetite is ruined with Gabriela."

"You will pay for this Dean. I swear you'll pay." Gabriela shakes her fist at Dean before she turns to me. Her dark eyes are now blood red and her face is drawn up as she starts to yell at me. I haven't seen her so upset before. She's normally pretty nice, for a bitch. "And for you, Angelica. You messed with me for the last time and Nicholas will hear about this. I'll make damn sure he knows what you've done." Joy, here she goes again threatening by telling dad something about me again. It isn't the first time and I'm sure it won't be the last time. Dean steps in front of her and cuts her off from yelling anymore at me. He is impressing me today by first standing up for Bethany and now for me. I agree to eat with him after Gabriela storms out of the restaurant, making sure everyone hears her leave.

Dean

I can't believe how much different Angelica looks outside of work. Her cheeks aren't as red as they normally are at work so she must not be wearing any make-up at all. Her skin looks like a newborn baby's skin though. It's smooth all over and doesn't look like she's seen any pain in her life. Her face looks innocent and that makes her so attractive. I love how she isn't wearing a mask to cover her thoughts and feelings. She isn't afraid to show who she really is and isn't hiding a ton of secrets.

"So, what do you recommend?" I want her to feel more comfortable with me, but I'm not sure that will ever happen. I can tell she hates Gabriela and that they've known each other for a while. I want to ask more about how they know each other, but I also don't want her running off. It feels great having her next to me once again. I've missed her.

"Everything is great, Jose is working today, and he cooks great." I can tell she is still nervous about eating with me. I'm nervous also.

"You don't have to eat with me if I make you feel uncomfortable." I grin at her trying to get her to smile at me.

"I am very uncomfortable." She tucks a small strand

of hair behind her ear. "Why do you want to eat with me and not Gabriela or someone like your friend Bethany?" By the question I know she thinks she doesn't measure up to the way they look, but she's wrong, dead wrong.

"I like the company I have right now. I thought Gabriela liked me, but I know she was wanting to use me to hurt you. And Bethany is a friend. I'm not going to lie, there was one night that we were more than friends but that's in the past."

"Oh." Angelica starts to shift her weight to stand up.

"Please don't leave. You look worn out and tried. Take a break and eat with me. Then if you still don't talk or spend time with me, we won't see each other again. Please." I try not to sound desperate, but she looks so worn out from working. I guess being the boss takes a lot out of you.

"Ok. Only because I want to see how the staff interacts with the costumers and how well they do serving." She grins and tries to hide any of her emotions. I don't care if that's the real reason or not, I'm just happy she is staying.

Angelica was not lying when she said Jose could cook. I think he could make an old shoe taste good. The food is the best I've ever had and the service wasn't bad. Bethany came by to apologize to

Angelica and to turn in her stuff. I guess she thought she was going to be fired before her first day was over. Angelica told her it was ok and explained that Gabriela is sometimes a bitch. She made it clear though that nothing like that could ever happen again. She also said that Gabriela has a way to poison everything around her.

"Why do you say Poison?" I've heard her say that before but I don't understand why.

"Gabriela has a way to draw you in close with her charm and good looks, but then she strikes. She bites you and won't let go. Then she releases a poison that runs through your veins and it makes you only focus on her." Angelica's face drops and her eyes fill with water as she fights back tears.

"I'm, sorry for asking? I didn't know." I try to plead with her but nothing I say changes the look she has on her face. I'm not sure what I'm apologizing for, but it feels like the right thing to do.

"No, you don't know. Not many people do." A tear falls from her eye as she reaches for her drink. "I've never seen anyone turn her down for me before. Normally, I'm last." The desire in her voice makes me think that she knows Gabriela in more than just as a boss.

"How do you know her?" I ask without thinking. Her

face turns red and she drops her head. She doesn't
want to answer, I know that, but I want to know.

"Gabriela is my-." Her eyes shoot up to the sound of
footsteps getting closer.

"What's going on?" A man in a dark business suit is
standing at our table yelling at Angelica. "Why did
you kick Gabriela out? You have no right to treat her
like that."

"Dad, let me explain." Angelica stands up and starts
to open her mouth.

"You've always been jealous of her, always. Why
can't you just leave her alone?" Angelica's dad is,
Nicholas? Gabriela threaten she would call him, but I
wasn't expecting him to be her dad. But why would
he believe Gabriela and not his own daughter?

"Dad, that's not what happened." Angelica starts
raising her voice at her father and he snaps an evil
stare at her.

"Don't you dare yell at me! Who do you think you
are?" I've only met this guy for five seconds and I'm
ready to bust him in his head. Why is he being such a
jerk to her?

"Sir, if I may." I step in between the two of them. "I
came here tonight with Gabriela for dinner, she
started yelling at one of the waitresses and then at

your daughter. I asked Angelica to have dinner with me instead of Gabriela because of the way she was acting." The man turns and has hate in his eyes as he shifts his weight to his back foot.

"So, you're the one she's been fucking? Now that you're done with one, you think you can have the next one. My daughter? You think you can have any woman you want?" Before I realize what happened, I have a surge of pain shooting through my nose. The white tablecloths around me are speckled with red blood as it spills from my nose and onto the marble flooring. I didn't see it coming. Angelica's dad isn't a big guy, thank God, but he's my height with maybe less than a hundred pounds than I weigh. I think of attacking him, but the look on Angelica's face says it all.

"Dad!" She yells as she runs to me. "What the hell is wrong with you?" I, really, don't like her dad now. "Gabriela has you believing whatever she wants you to. Why can't you see that? It was the same before mom died."

Angelica's father sinks down to a chair and covers his face. I can barely see him weeping due to the swelling. Damn, that guy has a punch.

"Dean, are you ok?" Angelica is cleaning the blood that's still coming from my nose with a napkin. Everyone in the restaurant is on their feet watching the commotion.

"I'm fine. I think my nose is broken though. But other than that, I am fine." I still want to jump up and beat the shit out of the old man. What is his fucking problem? He thinks I'm falling in love with his daughter and his response is to punch me? Or did he think she's going to be the next girl I bend over?

"What is your problem dad?" Angelica shoots him a stare to kill. Her eyes are not a bright blue like the cool waters but harden with hate. A look that can pierce your soul. "Why do you always believe her and never me? I am your daughter. She was just the whore you married."

Angelica

Two years ago, dad wanted me to work for him to start learning about the businesses he owned. I didn't care anything about them but I know mom would have wanted us to make up. She always told me that it wasn't easy when dad left her but one day I would have to forgive him. She knew there were reasons why he left but never said them. She only said that they couldn't see eye to eye on her research.

I dad I didn't want anything to do with her and that I hate him and Gabriela. Dad is trying to get me to be near him for some reason. After eight years, he wants me back in his life. Why now? When he ran off with Gabriela, I wanted nothing to do with him or that whore. I remember mom crying herself to sleep at night after he left. And now. After all this time. He wants me to come work for her. He must be crazy.

"You can do any job you want there. You can work in the office. Just name it."

I think about telling him no and just hanging up. Dad never calls anymore, so for him to call out of the blue was odd. He's probably up to something? "I will come and work there. But. I have my conditions."

"Anything you want. I just want you back in my life dear. I love you." Now I know he's up to something.

Dad hasn't talked to me like that in years. I know he wants something, but the question is, what?

"I will work there if I can work in the archives room. I think mom would've liked that." He agrees, a little too fast. So, I add another stipulation. "Also, I don't want to have to take orders from Gabriela. I don't want her to threaten my job or anything like that. I don't care that you were married to her or still are or whatever. She isn't my mom or stepmom and she'll never be."

"Honey, you have my promise. Gabriela and I are over anyways and in the divorce, I agreed to let her own some businesses. It was the cheapest way to do things. But I still own the pharmaceutical place, so your position there will be just fine."

I should've never agreed and let dad talk me into working for him or that whore. Both are up to something, but I just don't know what. He says they are divorced but they are always together.

Dean

What? He's married to that crazy bitch? So, that's how Gabriela and Angelica know each other. No wonder he was mad at me, I had his wife and he thought I was going to have his daughter.

"Don't you see, she's playing you, like she always does? Just like before mom died." Angelica is still cleaning my nose and her dad won't turn to look at her.

"You've grown up. When did you grow up?" Nicholas is mumbling to himself.

"Yes dad, I have. I have always been in Gabriela's shadow until now. Dean wants to spend with me instead of her. Something that you never wanted to do. When she was around, you were worse than a dog in heat." I'm still in shock; not because of my nose but because Angelica and Gabriela are stepdaughter and mother. How did I miss it? Why didn't anyone tell me?

"I don't think I can run the restaurant, dad. Nor do I think I could go back Mullers. You own it, so if you want me to go back, then get rid of that bitch!" Angelica is yelling at her dad now.

"You agreed to work for her. I might own it, but she runs it." Angelica's dad is turning red in his face now. My head is spinning, trying to figure out what the hell is going on. No wonder Angelica told me that Gabriela can't fire her. Gabriela can't fire the owner's daughter.

"She runs it like her personal whore house and I'm finished. You didn't want me ten years ago and you sure to hell don't want me now." Angelica grabs my arm and leads me to the door. I still can't see very much and my damn nose fucking hurts.

We make it back to Angelica's place and she's packing everything of value up. She has a large suitcase and she's stuffing it with clothes, jewelry, and anything that isn't nailed down. I'll try and help her if she wants me to after the pain from my nose goes away though. I've never been punched before and it hurts. Normally I always see the punches coming, but I missed this one by a mile.

"Angelica, what are you doing?" I wipe the last bit of blood off the end of my nose and think it is good for a little while now. "You don't have to leave. I don't want you to leave." I take her by the hand and led her to the bed so we can talk. I want her to vent to me and get all of her frustrations out. I know she probably still hates me but I don't think I'm number one on her list anymore.

"It's been ten years. Ten fucking years since she died. And now, now he wants to play dad. He wants to-."

Tears are flowing down her cheeks as she buries her head in my shoulder. I hold on to her tight and know she misses her mom in times like this. Too many nights I remember crying for my mom or wishing that I could talk to her one more time. I know the pain she is feeling right now and it sucks.

"If you want, I can stay with you a few days and help you pack? Whatever you need, I can do it." I figure if I give her a few days maybe she'll cool down and change her mind about whatever it is she is about to do. I don't want to lose her. We have both lost so much in our lives and I want for one second, one damn second, we win. I want us to win this fight and have the universe be nice to us. Maybe she'll see that she can't run from her past. I've tried for years to run from mine and I still find myself drawn right back to it somehow. It's our destiny to suffer in life but if she runs from her dad now, she will just hurt more inside. Running won't make the pain go away or the nightmares stop. She will have to face her demon head-on and stand up for herself. She is stronger than she knows and I will be right there to help her along her way. I need to face my demons as well but I don't know where she is at the moment.

"Let me help you. I have some money that I can give you. It'll help you get by." No one knows that I still have close to the full settlement stashed away for when I need it. I didn't want to spend the money or even think of it because it hurts too much. But I would give it all to Angelica if she needed it.

"I don't want to take your money. Just be a good friend. Please. I need one right now." I want to be more than just a good friend to her. I want to be with her. I want to help her and hold her. I want to wipe away her tiers and make her forget about her pain. I want her to trust in me and me alone. I want her. I want. I want to tell her so much. I'm scared to tell her anything though. I have fucked two women that I didn't even know for no reason and now I am holding the girl of my dreams in my arms and all I can think about is spending the rest of my life with her.

Angelica

Dean doesn't know my past and I don't know if I'm ready to tell him about it yet or not. As I snuggle next to him in bed and let his strong arms hold me, I think of a year earlier when I thought I was in love.

"Hi, pumpkin." Richard is just getting home from work and I'm about to start my first, official day working for my dad. I've been living with Richard and his sister for a while now after mom died. At first, I was placed in a foster home for a few years and it was a hellish nightmare. I didn't like anyone, and I tried to keep to myself most of the time. One day, my foster dad went after his wife with a steak knife and I was removed from the home. That's when I meet Richard and his sister and my life changed for the better. I started living with them when I was fourteen and when I turned sixteen, Richard asked me to be his girlfriend. It was a little odd at first but we both had strong feelings for each other. I lived with him and his sister for years and he never gave me the slightest idea that he was attracted to me. I moved out on my own when I turned seventeen and got my own apartment. Richard and I stay close and we dated some, but nothing ever serious. He is eight years older than I am, and I don't think I'm ready for a boyfriend just yet. It's nice to have someone to talk to and share feelings with, though. But that's as far as it ever got with him. I know he wants me to be a different person but I'm not. I'm still the little lost girl he saved many years ago that is still having a hard time coping with her mother's death. His sister and I became very close and we still talk now and then. I miss her more than I miss him but she had a wild side that I could never be like. But she was the sweetest person in the world but her stories would make me cry laughing at how she manipulated men to do whatever she wanted them to do.

Dean is trying his hardest to get me to stay longer but I need to leave. This place makes me think of my dad too much and I don't want to think about him anymore. It's nice having Dean here with me and to have him to talk to. We both have been through so much and somehow, he coops with his loss better than I have. Richard and I stopped seeing each other the day after Dean's car exploded. We both knew the day was coming but he saw the way I looked at Dean and he knew it was over. Something about Dean drew me to him and I didn't feel right dating Richard and possibly have feelings for someone else and he knew it. My stomach turns to think that I have feelings for more than one person at a time. I don't think dad ever had feelings for my mom and Gabriela at the same time, but I wanted to end things with Richard before I ended up hurting him. I never told him how I really felt about him and I never answered him the other night.

I never thought that I would feel comfortable with a guy at my house, but there is something about Dean that makes it great. After the night he had with Gabriela, Dean thought it would be best to take off for a little while to let things blow over. I think he might have other reasons for taking off and it doesn't bother me either. I need someone to spend time with and Dean has been a great friend this week. A few nights we laid on the couch and fell asleep together. I've always heard stories of how fast guys like him are to get into your panties, but he hasn't made a move. I was kind of hoping he would but it took him forever to make his first move last time. I've never been with anyone and have never thought about sleeping with anyone, until Dean. Richard and I would never fall asleep together or lay around talking all night. He was all about work and thought that he needed to impress me all the time. I love laying with Dean and having his rock-hard body pressed against me as I sleep. I think he was sent back into my life to be my guardian angel and to protect me. Not sure if he is to save me from my past or help me with my future. But he seems perfect. Each morning he has breakfast waiting for me and every night he has something planned out for supper. He is perfect but I fear I'm missing the terror that is hiding around the corner as the week grows to an end. I want to know if Dean will stay with me and protect me or will he abandon me like my dad did? Every now and again he'll get weird phone calls at night and I try not to listen but it's hard not to hear his sexy voice.

"I told you no. I'm not doing it." I can hear him on the phone with someone in the living room. I told him I'm going to take a shower when I heard his phone ringing. I hate that he can't go do whatever it is he does on the weekends. I start running my water when I hear his voice get louder.

"I told you. I don't give a fuck how much money she is paying. NO!" He's screaming at the other person on the phone. He thinks I'm in the shower and can't hear him. I'm standing near the bedroom door, listening to him talk, or yell, at the person on the other end of the line.

"Fuck you then! I'm not doing it. That's final." I can see the back of Dean's head as he's pacing the floor in the living room, still yelling at cursing on the phone.

"It's none of your fucking businesses who I'm with, and you can tell her that I don't give a damn how much she'll pay. I'm not for sale." I've been listening to him talk for over five minutes and think I better get my shower before he starts to get suspicious.

Dean doesn't say much when I get out of the shower and he's dressed, holding his car key and wallet in his hand. The look on his face is more fear than anything else. I want to ask him what his phone call is about, but then again, I didn't want him to know I was listening.

Dean says he needs to go take care of something, I guess it has to do with his phone call, but he doesn't say. It isn't long before he comes walking back into the apartment but he seems to have changed in a matter of hours. Whatever it was he went to take care of has him shaken and he isn't the same Dean that I spent the week with. I know is hiding something but I don't know what. I search his face for answers but his eyes are cold and distant. I don't know if he is giving up on himself or giving up on me, but I wish he would talk to me. He looks lost and I wish he would be mine. I think I might be falling for him again and I want him to save me. I want him to be *my* knight that rides in on a white horse and rescues me. Why won't he just, *help me*. I know that I'm more of a burden than anything else to him and I need to stop portending. He tells me that he will do anything I want him to, I want him to be there for me. He said he would take care of me and protect me. I think the old Dean would have protected me but now he doesn't have the same conviction in his eyes as he did. Whatever his phone call was about, it's made him mad and I don't think he can deal with it with me around. I know what I need to do. Dean goes to get a shower and I think of what I need to do. I know in my heart what I should do but I don't think I am strong enough to do it.

Dean's phone beeps as soon as he turns on the water and I don't think much of it. It has been driving me crazy on how much it's been going off today but when it beeps a second time, I go to check it out.

Good. U needed to break all ties with her. Let me know how it goes.

BTW swing by after you dump her ass. We need to talk

I want to throw his phone out the window, but I don't want to be like my dad. But if he doesn't want to be with me, then that's fine.

"Dean, we need to talk." I walk into the bedroom to see what's taking him so long after I heard the water shut off. He said he needed to talk to me before he got in the shower and after reading his text message, I need to talk to him. He's been out of the shower for more than fifteen minutes but hasn't come out of the bedroom. I don't know why he is avoiding me tonight but I'm about to find out what's going on with him. He's standing in the bedroom near my suitcase wearing nothing but boxers. They aren't long boxers either and I didn't know they made them that short. They were shorter than the shortest pair of shorts I have.

"What's up?" He turns and smiles at me like nothing is wrong and nothing has been wrong all day. It's the old dean standing in front of me now. I am confused about what his mood swing has been today. My suitcase is open on the floor and he's walking away from it like there is a bomb in it. I think he's up to something, but I can't think with the way he is standing in front of me wearing nothing. I know he is wearing boxers but my mind is not thinking right now. I stand in amazement at his chiseled chest and ripples that cascade down his abs like a waterfall. He has the V. God, he has the V cut stomach. The come, take me V that I didn't know anyone in real life really had. My God he is HOT.

"Um." My tongue won't do what I want it to do right now. My mind is going a million miles an hour and I have never felt so hot before. My body is on fire as I look at him. I've never seen a man half-naked in front of me before and the worst part, he's in my bedroom. I think that's bad that's he's in my bedroom half-naked, but then again I'm really happy he's in my room. I move closer to him to tell him that I'm leaving and he can't do anything to stop me. I'm going to tell him that I'm leaving in the morning but the scent of his body hits my nose and my legs go

numb. I have a tightening feeling between my legs
that I have never before. I'm wearing gym-style
shorts and a tank with no bra, I hate dressing up, but
now I fear Dean can tell I'm getting turned on. I
know he has to see that my nipples are aroused
already. I tell my legs to turn and run out of the room
but they are betraying me right now. I keep telling
them to work but they aren't listening to me. The rest
of my body is following suit as I stand there, stunned
by the gorgeous god of man in my room. My feet feel
heavy like they are stuck in concrete and I can't
move. My heart is racing as Dean slowly walks
toward me. He's comfortable in his body and he
doesn't shy away from it one bit. I, on the other hand,
am blushing enough for the both of us but he stops in
the middle of the room, staring at me, searching my
face for a reaction. I came into the bedroom to tell
him that I was leaving. I thought I would give him
the space he needs so I won't be a burden to him any
longer. But how can I leave this man? The
conviction in his eyes right now is strong enough to
start a fire on water. I start to open my mouth again,
but my words are lost.   "What is it you wanted to
tell me?" My God his voice is as sexy as his body.
What am I doing? Angelica, snap out of it. He is just
a man. A very, very, very hot man. A man that can
do all kinds of nasty things to me and I will let him
with pleasure. His soft voice falls like raindrops on
my ears. I can't move. I can't speak. I feel myself

getting wet and I know he'll see my shorts soaked at any movement. I've never felt like this before. Is this even normal? Am I turning into one of those girls that gets flustered every time they see a hot guy? I'm strong. I'm brave. I'm-. I'm-. I'm yours. Take me.

"I. I. I need you." My words are betraying me now. What the hell is wrong with me? Speak dammit. It's English, I've spoken it my entire life. My mind won't get Dean's hot body fucking me out of it long enough to say what I want it to. He grins as he leans down to my forehead and kisses it slowly. What is he doing? Oh, God. His lips just touch my skin. His soft, wet lips, just touch my skin. Why? Why did he do that? I feel like screaming to him, *I'm yours, all yours! Do what you want to me!* His arms wrap around my waist as he moves from my head to my lips. No! No! Don't do this. Don't touch my lips with your soft lips. Aw. His tongue flicks the inside of my mouth as he wraps his arms around me. I'm off the ground and pressed against his body. I tell my mind to fight this urge and to be stronger than the rest of my body.

"No. We shou-." My tongue won't work now as Dean's tongue flicks the tip of mine. He is so much stronger than I am and my body is giving up. I don't want this to come between us but I want him. I want him all for me. If I'm going to be another nautch in on his belt then he can stop right now. But if he wants me the same way I want him, then this happen. I've heard the first time hurts but I don't care right now. My body should be punished for disobeying me and I want Dean to punish all of me. I'm ready for the pain, if the pleasure is as intense as I've already experienced then I'm ready.

I know I'll scream at the top of my lungs when he enters me but I don't care. I want him deep inside my wetness. I need him to be with me. I need him this close to me like no one has been before. I'm his and he can do what he wants to me. I, am, his.

He lifts me like feathers as he carries me to the bed. I'm weightless, floating through the air as he carries his prey to feast on. His sweet kisses go from my mouth to my neck and his tongue is a whirlwind of pleasure. I can't control myself anymore as I feel a new aching between my legs.

I don't understand why people this isn't nice or they don't enjoy themselves during sex. Dean's hard body presses against mine and all I can think about is how he'll feel inside me. I'm scared to know how he'll feel though as I know must be large. My arms are above my head and Dean's hands are sliding up my shirt. His hands are soft and strong as they make their way to my breast. His finger traces my nipple as he kisses my neck. I let out a small moan as his mouth goes from my neck to my nipple. His tongue teases and plays with me as his hand cups my breast. My hands are still above my head and my shirt is making its way to my fingertips. When it reaches them, I toss it to the floor, not caring that I'm topless under Dean's pleasure. My mind starts to wonder how many other women have been in this same position with him. How many other women did Dean take their innocents away from? My hands find his head and I pull his hair as he continues to pull at my nipple. Pain shots through my body and down through my body. With every pull, I moan louder. I want him. I don't care how many other women there were before me, Dean makes me feel like I'm the only one left in the world right now.

"I need you, Dean. I need you, now." I moan as his hands hold my back while he takes my entire breast in his mouth. "Oh, oh. Dean." I moan more. I've never felt pleasure like this before. Why did I wait so long to have sex before? Is this what it always feels like? I want to lock myself in my room with Dean for the next 40 years and just enjoy this moment over and over again.

I can feel something large on my leg coming from behind Dean's boxers. Every time I scream, it throbs a little more. I've seen pictures of men before, but I want what Dean has inside me.

"Please, Dean. Please." I beg him to enter me and take this painful pleasure away so he can replace it again and again.

"Not yet." Not yet? Not yet? Are you serious? What is he doing to me? Is he trying to kill me or something? I thought there was sex and that's it. What else could be doing? His hands move down my back, pulling my hips in the air as I feel my shorts slide down my legs and hear them crash to the floor. They must have weighed 100 pounds because now my legs are free to move anyway Dean wishes them to.

"Oh, God." I bite my lip as his kisses trace a line down my stomach to where my fire is building inside. What is he planning on doing down there? "OH!" I scream out as his tongue hits my wet, innocent middle. His strong hands have my ass cupped as his tongue tantalizes every sensation I have as he squeezes me in tighter to his mouth.

"Oh my God, Angelica." He moans as his tongue goes in and out of my wetness and then back across to the spot that has been making my toes curl and my back arch.

"Oh, OH!" I scream louder as my legs want to squeeze his head with the sensation that's being shot through my body but resist. I want to release this pleasure that is building inside me though but I don't want him to stop. "Please Dean, Please. I want to feel. OH! OH! YOU!" My mouth won't work as his mouth covers me again and he breaths, taking all of

me in his mouth. "OH FUCK!" I can't help but
scream as the fire is raging out of control. I try not to
say fuck too or around too many people. My mom
hated that word with a passion but it is one bad habit
that I picked up from my dad. Richards sister, on the
other hand, used it all the time. She always told me
that when a man finally turns me into a woman, that I
would be screaming it from the top of my lungs. She
wasn't lying because right now I don't know another
word to use. The bottled-up painful pleasure that he's
giving me is about to explode like a volcano erupting.
One of Dean's hands moves from my back to the
center of the fire. Somehow his tongue is still licking
me as he enters with his finger. A shot of excitement
soars through my body as his finger hits my G-spot.
I'm in tears from the pleasure, but I want more. I let
out some more fucks as he works his finger in and
out, licking and sucking me at the same time.

"Come for me, baby. Let yourself go." What is he
talking about?

I don't understand, come?

"OHHH, holy fucking hell!" I scream as I know what
he means now. My body quivers as I tighten and
throb at Dean's finger starts rubbing me faster. The
fire that was burning has just been extinguished by
him and it feels like I've been running for ten miles.

"Now are you ready for me?" Dean whispers with a

grin as he slips his boxers off. My mouth drops as his cock flops out like a sea monster.

"Holy shit!" There are no words to describe what I'm looking at and I haven't seen anything like this to compare him too. His cock is the same size or larger than my arm and I don't know what he plans on doing with it. "Where is that going?" I sincerely say as he lowers himself down on me.

"This might hurt a little." Dean whispers as he reaches for a condom in his jeans pocket.

"No, I'm on the pill. I want my first time to be without a condom." I say as I push the condom out of his hand. I want my first time to be special and I don't want to be just another girl for him. I've been on the pill for a few years now to keep my period more regular. I never thought it would come in handy for a day like today but I want to feel all of Dean with no restrictions. I don't want him to hold anything back and I don't care about how many women he has been with or what.

"Trust me. This might hurt. But trust me." Dean slowly lowers himself down on my and I feel him slowly push inside me.

He slowly enters my body with his massive self my eyes shut fast from the pain. The head slowly goes in and he stops. "Does that hurt?"

"No. God no. It feels great. I want more." I beg for him to push all the way inside me. I don't care if it's going to hurt I want it. I let out a scream as he pushes deeper, and my legs shake at his size. God does it hurt. "Oh," I scream in pleasure as he slowly goes deeper.

"Holy fuck, you're so tight." Dean whispers as he pushes as deep as he can inside me. He feels great and I scream a few more times until my body gets used to him inside me. I wrap my legs around his waist and try to pull him in deeper but he is already as deep as he can be. I feel his body slam into mine as his rhythm stuffs me with his large rode. This is what I want.

"Oh. YES! OH, fuck yes!" I take his screaming as a sign of approval and I smile as he starts to shake all over. I know I'll be sore in the morning, but I don't care. I don't care if I can't walk for a week, I just don't want this night to end.

He starts pounding me hard and I can feel him up to my neck each time. I try to bite a pillow but he pulls it away and pounds me harder. He smiles every time he slams into me. How does my body take this abuse? Oh, it feels great and I want more. "Pound me harder." I cry for him to never stop.

I can feel the pleasure building again and I know I'm going to explode like I did with his finger but more intensely this time.

"I'm going to... AW! Come! Again!" My voice is shaky as he slows his pounding to allow me to explode. I think I'm going to break him in half with how much I squeeze down on him. He curses and yells as I feel him explode inside me. This must be his release; good Lord I didn't expect it to be so much.

"Stay here. Don't leave tonight." Dean says as he rolls off me and holds onto me tight from behind. I'm drunk from his love and I want it every night. I know this is only for tonight and that tomorrow I will leave. I can't stay and it isn't fair to him.

We fall asleep in bed, wrapped around each other, intertwined as we sleep. I want to stay here forever but I know it can't last.

Dean

After we made love, we fell asleep together and I've never fallen asleep with a girl, ever. Even the times I've spent with Roxanna we never just slept together. After I would bag them, I would leave, or they would leave. If they did stay the night, we normally end up fucking all night long. Angelica is different though, I don't want to keep going all night with her. I want to save my time with her and be part of her in more than just sex.

I wake to her beauty standing by the window. She's wearing my shirt and nothing else and she doesn't look as innocent now. She went from a girl to a woman and I made her that way. Her skin is glowing from the morning sun and she looks at peace.

"Good morning." I smile at her but she doesn't smile back.

"I have to leave." She says it real low like she is questioning herself or convincing herself, I'm not sure yet. But she's looking out the window, at the world outside.

"What are you talking about? What do you mean you have to leave? No, you don't. You can stay here. We can stay together." My words come out like a dam bursting open. I'm falling for her? Why does

118

she think she must leave? We can make a life together, here or anywhere, it doesn't matter. I need her. I want her. I've tasted the sweet nectar that she has, and I want to bathe in it every night. "Don't leave. I have money. I can support you and me both." She doesn't move from her spot at the window as she stares, frozen in time. I hear a ding and she looks down at her phone in her hand.

"I have to leave. It's the only way you'll be safe." She turns and looks at me with tears in her eyes. "You must let me go." She's searching for a reason to let me go, for me to let her go, but why? Why does she need to push me away? Is she trying to protect me from someone or is she protecting herself? Who is making her this scared? Is it her dad, Gabriela, or someone else? Who? I don't need protection. I can protect us both. I'll die for her to keep her safe.

"I'm not going to let you leave." I keep repeating as I jump out of bed. She's not going anywhere without a fight. I'm not losing her like I did my parents.

Angelica

"Angelica don't leave. I'm sure we can figure this out." Dean's trying to get me to stay and live with him. He says he has an extra room and he has a lot of money in the bank. Money isn't an issue for me though. My mom made sure I had all I needed before she died. She left me millions in different accounts that my dad or Gabriela didn't know about, so they couldn't touch it or try to take it away from me.

"I can't." I want to trust Dean and I want him to be the one that I love one day, but how can I trust him. I trusted my dad once but he let me down. When mom got sick and everyone turned their backs on me. Doctors told me there wasn't any way to help her but they wouldn't even try. No one wanted to help. She had a friend that was always there for her. One that always stood up for mom no matter what. That's what a true friend does and she was an angel sent to protect mom. But even angels fall sometimes and God needs them to come back to heaven. She died shortly before mom got sick and no one was ever sent to replace her job in my mom's life.

"I can't let you leave. Where will you go?" Dean's blocking the door and tries to stop me. His large frame is taking up the whole doorway as he stands tall, trying not to let me pass. He slips his boxers back on and is trying his best to prevent me from leaving. I bite my jaw to keep from tackling him and make him replay last night.

Dean is wanting to know where I'm headed and what I'm going to do when I get there. The truth is, I don't know yet. I figure I'll go back home. I want to go back to where the accident happened and try to start over again. I keep replaying last night over in my head as I try to find a flaw in him. I want to make this easier and not like I'm abandoning him. I think back to the text that I received this morning and the text Dean had last night. Everything makes sense now. I know I should stop pretending and start facing the truth. There's no way I can have Dean the way he wants me. If he even wants me. I know he is saying it now, but it's just because of last night. What will he do when he's tired of me? Will he toss me to the side like all the other women?

"I don't know yet." I lie to him. I know now where I am going but I am not telling him. I'm going back to the house I took care of mom in. I know that much for sure but what I do after I get there; I don't know yet. I'm leaving Orlando and I don't want anyone to follow me. Dad surely has forgotten about the house. He forgot about everything else after the accident, so it would make sense he would forget that as well. "Dean, I need time to think. Please let me leave. No one loves me here. There, there isn't anything here for me anymore. I can't be dad's little princess that answers to Gabriela."

"Why does your dad still let her run his life? She isn't with him anymore." Dean tries to make me feel better but remembering him being her boy toy and makes me mad at him even more. Now he had me as well, another notch in his belt. Is that how men are controlled? Can they be made to do whatever the hell you want by just having sex with them? Men are pigs.

"I told you. She's poison. When her venom seeps into your veins, you can't let go. She owns you and controls you." Why can't he see her for who she is? But why do I have to push Dean away?   Is there another way? I'm so confused right now. The only way that he can be safe is if I leave, but he makes me feel special. Last night he made me feel more than just special; he made me feel wonderful. But I'm afraid Gabriela will come back for him. This time, she might hurt him. Especially if she knows I care for him. I don't think he cares for me the same way though. I tell him I'm leaving because no one loves me. He never says he does. He never says he cares for me. Nothing. He just stands there with a blank expiration on his face.

"I want you here, isn't that enough to keep you from leaving?" It's sweet that he's begging but he doesn't want me, he wants easy sex. He wants fake women and ones that know how to please him. It was the heat of the moment for him. I must make him let me go.

"You say that now, but you'll go back to her. They always do." I step up on my tippy toes and kiss Dean on the cheek. "Thanks for helping me pack and realizing that I need to leave." He stops fighting and steps to the side so I pass by him. I think my kiss delivered the knock blow I have been trying to land all morning to him. He's done now. Every emotion in his eyes is gone. Every emotion in his face has left. There's nothing there. He's dead inside and I made him that way. I expected him to fight tooth and nail for me. Maybe I want him too. Maybe I want him not to give up on me. I'm not strong enough to fight by myself but I want him to show me that he loves me like I love him. I look up at him, hoping that he will get mad and fight for me. If he fights for me I won't leave. I'll stay. I'll have to stay. I love Dean. Maybe I wish he'll sweep me off and my feet and take me to bed and show me he wants me. I want him to show me he wants last night again. The whole time I'm pleading with my eyes he just stands there and doesn't move. "Thank you for last night." I kiss his lips and slide my shorts on and keep the shirt that I stole from him and start walking out the front door. I'm packed and ready to leave even though I don't want to. I want him to run after me. I want him to want me, to show me that he wants me. I leave him standing in the doorway of my old apartment as I head north.

Dean

I want to stop her from leaving and wrap my arms around her. I want to hold her tight until she realizes I need her. She's hurting and I did nothing. I didn't do a damn thing. I stood there and watched her get in her car and drive away. Why? Why didn't I stop her? I'm supposed to help her, but I let her go. I do nothing as I watch as her car drives out of sight. "I already miss you." I say as a tear falls down my cheek. Why didn't I tell her how I felt? Why didn't I fight harder for her?

I stand in the doorway, hoping that when she gets to the end of the block she'll turn around. I know she's not coming back and I don't blame her. I did nothing to try and keep her from leaving but her mind was already made up. I pull my phone out to check what time it is. She's gone from my life and I must take care of something today.

Good. U needed to break all ties with her. Let me know how it goes.

BTW swing by after you dump her ass. We need to talk

I hadn't realized Lorenzo text me last night. We've been talking about Gabriela and I told him that I was through with that bitch. She called the club and told

Lorenzo that she would pay 20K if I would come and do a party for her. I've known him for a long time and have his fingers into everything. So when someone offers him money to get something done, he will try any favors he might have to make it work. He was mad as hell though when I told him to go fuck himself. I told him how I felt about Angelica and that I hadn't had feelings like this since Roxanna. He knew I was serious, and he understood.

Me- Heading over there in a few to tell her I quit

Lorenzo- About damn time. So you and this Angelica chick good?

Me- No. She left this morning and wouldn't tell me where. I feel worse now than when Roxanna left

Lorenzo- You know she's coming back right.

Just found out.

Might be a few weeks, who knows with her

Me- Bullshit

Quit trying to fuck with me

Lorenzo- no bullshit

I'll tell you more when I see you

Lorenzo has been full of shit ever since I knew him, but this time, I think he's telling the truth. Now I'm really fucked.

I drive to Mullers to turn in my, I quit notice. I'm done with them and don't care if I ever find out the truth about my parents or not. I just let the best thing in my life drive away because I didn't want to see her hurting anymore. This was the second time I've done that in my life and I will never do it again.

I see Gabriela's car in the parking lot once I pull in. "Good. I need to talk to her." I say to no one. I walk past everyone and don't stop on the way to tell the front desk girl what was going on; I see Gloria but I walk past her as well. I am on a warpath and am looking for one person. "Gabriela," I call out as I walk into her office without knocking.

"Dean. What the hell are you doing? Do you think that since your fucking the owner's daughter that gives you the right to do whatever the fuck you want now?" Gabriela is with a client and they are watching with aw as I never stumble over my words with her.

"You listen here you bitch. I will talk to you, how, the fuck ever, I fucking, want to. And you want to know why? Cause I don't give a fucking shit about you or this damn place. I hope you burn in hell and take that fucking dick, Nicholas, there with you. Angelica left because of you. Because you were jealous of our friendship. If you're not on top, then you aren't happy. Take this job and go fuck yourself with it." Before she can make a sound, I turn around and head back out her door. I don't wait for a response as I head out the door with my head held high.

God that felt good. I think as I walk to my car. I've never talked to anyone like that before and always took whatever was thrown my way. My parents taught me to always be respectful and polite, but I think they are smiling down on me for this one. The look on her face before I turned and walked out was priceless and I wish I had it on camera. She didn't know what hit her. I'm leaving and I don't care who knows what's going on. I need to stop by the club and talk to Lorenzo in person and then it's off to find Angelica.

When I arrive at the club, Lorenzo is outside waiting on me. I text him and told him I was on my way when I left after telling Gabriela off.

"I'm done." I don't have to say anything else. He knew that long before this point and was glad to see me finally going in the right direction.

"I know. I know. It sucks. But I know." He grabs the back of his neck and rubs his large hand back and forth. He's searching for a way to tell me something that he doesn't want me to hear. I know it's about

Roxanna. "She's coming back. Soon." He's still rubbing his neck as he looks down at the ground. He doesn't have to say her name, he knows I know who he's talking about. "She asked about you. I didn't get to speak to her, but she was told that you were done, we all knew it long before now."

My heart sank at the feeling of Roxanna maybe hurting because she thought that after all these years there may still be something between us. "Yeah. I've found the one." I lean against my car and watch as he shifts his weight from one foot to the other.

He lets out a heavy sigh. "She wants to see you."

I don't want to hear it. I know she probably does, and a part of me wants to see her. I can't see her though. She left and hasn't spoken to me in years and now she wants to walk back into my life. No. "I'm heading north tonight. I've got to find Angelica. Last time I made a mistake by letting Roxanna walk out and I didn't chase her down. But this time. This time it's different."

Lorenzo walks over and gives me a hug. "Gonna miss the hell out of you."

"Don't lie." We both laugh and hug again and he turns to head back into the club. I know the next few days are going to be the hardest of my life and if Lorenzo's right and Roxanna is coming back to talk to me. My life is going to be even more complicated.

Angelica

I start driving north and never look back. My past is behind me and I need to keep my head up high and keep moving. I'm heading to the gulf and I'm not waiting for anyone. Mom had a small house at Sapphire Coast, close to Pensacola, and I'm heading there to drown out everything that had to do with dad and Dean. I don't want to see dad ever again and I want to see Dean but I'm not sure he wants the same thing. Dad is dead to me and mom is more alive than he ever could be. He isn't coming back in my life after all these years and expects me to just love him like I did a long time ago.

After eight hours of driving, I pull in at my mom's old house. It still looks like it did when I last saw it 10 years ago. She had a maid that was hired to keep the house clean and livable all these years; I remember something about it in the Will, and the house looks beautiful. Mom owned a few different businesses but when she got sick, she sold or traded some of them to make sure I had money to live on. I told her not to do it, but she wouldn't listen. She has been keeping her family name alive for over a hundred years and I didn't want to be the cause of them not being a family business anymore. But she wanted to make sure that dad didn't get anything. She told me that he skipped out and doesn't deserve anything that was hers. Mom

thought that one day I might come back to the beach
house when I was old enough and she thought right.
Now that I am ready to face the house again, it's time
to take on the town as well. The last time I was here,
mom was sick, and no one knew what happened or
how she got so sick from the accident. The other
people involved in the accident died right away, but
mom lived for a little while.

I pull my suitcase out and find something to slip on to
walk down to the beach. I've always loved the beach.
Something about the water calls me and draws me in
closer to the water. The smell of the water hits my
nose like a breath of fresh air. The waves crash
against the shoreline, washing my sadness away and
pulling them back out to sea. Nothing's better than
listening to this. The cool sand between my toes
tickles my feet as I walk ever so closer to utopia.
Mom and I would sit on the beach for hours and hours
watching the waves roll in. She would tell me stories
of pirates and lost treasures as we watch the moon rise
over the water. We never had a worry in the world as
we watched the water. I am always at peace when
I'm around water and I think of mom as I remember
her sweet voice and warm touch. I can't wait to get
down there to let go of everything. I pull out some
clothes to see what I want to wear but I don't have
much to choose from. Shorts and tanks were my
normal attire and I would wear sundresses but nothing

like you'd expect Florida girl to have. My whole
wardrobe cost as much as one outfit of Gabriela's.

"What the hell?" I gasp as I notice an envelope with
my name on it stuck in with the clothes. "Where did
this come from? Did Dean put it in here?"

"Angelica.

*I know you think that I will leave you when you need
me most. I've made that mistake once but I won't
ever do it again. I don't know if you are the one or
not. All I know, is I care for you. I want to make sure
you eat and you have some money to get on your feet.
It's not much but it's some. I know it's hard to start
over and I know how hard it is to lose someone you
love. I lost my parents ten years ago in a freak
accident and there isn't a day I don't think about them.
If you ever need anything or if you're lonely. Call me.
I know you need time to think and I am willing to give
you some time. Take care and I miss you. Always.*
Dean"

Tears fall from my eyes when I finish the letter. Dean didn't know me, but he thought I was starting fresh and with no money. Maybe he does care about me. Maybe I'm wrong about him. I open the envelope that's under the letter.

"A hundred thousand dollars!" I scream out loud. He gave someone that he barely knew a hundred thousand dollars to make sure they get back on their feet. I can't hold back my tears as the dam breaks and my face is soaked with emotion. My heart aches as I realize how much of a mistake I just made. Maybe he does love me, wait not maybe, I know he loves me. Oh, my God. I'm too stupid and caught up with my dad to see it.

I pull my phone out and dial his number. I'm telling him that I love him. I'm telling him that I want him. Oh, my God. There is so much I need to tell him right now.

"Hello?" A young girl answers the phone with a slow laugh. "He's all tied up sweetheart." She giggles again and then she hangs up.

Something doesn't sound right and I know Dean wouldn't have another girl lined up that fast after me. We had a connection and I know he felt it also. We've always had one but I think it's stronger now than ever. Why would Dean give me a hundred grand and then blow me off like this? I want to know what this phone sex sounding whore has done with the love of life. I dial him again.

"Damn. Voicemail." I stare at my phone trying to think of someone that would know Dean and would know if this sounds like him or not. Something must be wrong. It must. He wouldn't do this to me.

"Bethany!" I yell out loud as I frantically search my phone looking for her number. I remember Dean saying that they were friends, even though I think they might be a little more than just friends, but who cares right now. She should know if this sounds like him or not.

"Bethany. This is Angelica." I yell as soon as I hear her answer the phone. It only rang once before she answered and she sounded chipper and excited that I called her. She has a very sweet voice, a little too high pitch for my taste, but then again I'm not into girls.

"Oh my God. How are you Angelica? Where are you? Have you eaten? I have a ton of questions for you girl. But first. Have you talked to Dean? He called earlier and was wanting to know if I've heard from you and if you were ok. He said to call him as soon as I hear from you. I should call him right now." Bethany's full of energy and talking a mile a minute as I try to interrupt her. That girl likes to talk and I think she likes to hear her own voice just as much.

"I'm fine. I tried calling Dean and he didn't answer so don't waste your time. Some girl answered and said he was tied up." I try to disguise my voice and make it sound like I haven't been bawling my eyes out. I don't know why I feel the need to make her think I'm stronger than I am. I hate the thought of Dean already being with someone else.

"That doesn't sound like him. I heard he quit and told Gabriela to go fuck herself." Now I'm starting to panic; something doesn't seem right. Is someone trying to play an evil prank on me or is Dean in trouble?

"I am going to call Detective Moore. He's an old friend of mine. Maybe he can go by and check on him for me." I know I might be adding fuel to a fire by calling him, but I need to know that Dean is ok.

"Don't worry Angelica, I'm sure he's ok. He seems head over heels for you, so don't think the worst." I know Bethany is trying to make me feel better, but I've fallen for Dean. He can't be in trouble. If he isn't with some girl by choice; then why did one answer his phone? "I'll go by his house also. I'll call you if I find anything out." I'm glad she is going to check on him too. I hang up so I can call Detective Moore, I think he might be able to help me.

Detective Moore said that he would go by and check on Dean to see if he could find him. He said that if

Dean was there fucking another girl then he would shoot him on the spot and I wouldn't have to ever think of him again. I laugh, he's always been protective but I also know he isn't joking.

Angelica

After the night Dean and I had experienced together, I was ready to give him my life. I felt connected to him in ways that I never thought was possible. He was able to take all my fears and worries, roll them into a big ball and throw them out the window. Last night I knew without a shadow of doubt Dean was the man that I was going to love for the rest of my life. The only question is does he love me the same? His text last night plays in my mind and I should have just talked to him about it but I was afraid to know the truth. I was going to tell him about this place my mom had and the money she left for me but I just couldn't. Something about him makes me love him and hate him at the same time. I'm torn inside to think that he might love me but yet he might not. He gave me so much money without a second thought and then he watched me walk out the front door. He let me walk out of his life maybe forever and he acted like it never bothered him at all.

Dad tried to get everything he could when mom died, but she was able to hide some money from him to make sure I could live a good life. He was a greedy bastard that was only interested in money and easy women. He didn't show up to the funeral or check on me for years until he wanted something from me. Mom knew he wouldn't take care of me and that I would have to work for what I wanted. If dad found out about the house and money, he would try to take it all back. He was in love with Gabriela and she was sucking up everything he had. Dad never thought that after they married, Gabriela would sleep around with anyone that had money or she thought she could manipulate. He didn't have her sign a prenup, so when she left him, she took half of everything. She played him for a fool and I thought it was funny when I read about it in the papers. It pissed me off that she was taking what should have gone to me, but I didn't want anything that dad owned. His lawyers thought that if they paid her enough money she would leave him alone. The only catch, and the only good thing he ever did for me, was tell Gabriela she had to hire me and be nice. He made sure that after all these years I was taken care of. I don't know what changed in him, but it was nice to have my dad back. Even if it was for just a little while.

I didn't care if Gabriela was married to my dad, she was not my mom in the least. She called mom bad names every time I would mention her name around her. She hated mom with a passion and I never understood why. Mom was the nicest person in the world and wouldn't hurt a fly. She loved her job and helping people. Dad said that I was like her in so many ways and that's why he didn't want to be around me for all those years. He admitted that he

gave up the best woman ever for a greedy bitch and I
make sure I remind him of it every chance I get.
Mom and Gabriela worked together and that's how
dad met her. It started out as fun flirting at the office
that soon turned into late nights working on reports
together.

Mom began to be suspicious of dad going to the office
at night and not being home when she got home.
Gabriela was also mom's assistant, but mom couldn't
find her a lot of the time. She told me that dad
changed and when the accident happened, he went to
Gabriela. Mom didn't try to stop him because she
knew what would happen if she tried to step in.
Gabriela made it clear that she would not stop until
dad was hers and mom feared she would destroy me if
she had the chance too.

Gabriela sent me a message this morning that she
would take Dean like she did my dad. She said that if
I cared for him in any way, then I would let him go.
She threatened me like she did mom and she was
enjoying it. She didn't want Dean and it was clear
that Dean didn't want her, but she wanted to take him
from me. I wanted to protect Dean and keep him safe
from her poison and the only thing I could. Leave.

My heart aches as I think of the card and money that
Dean left for me. He loves me more than he knows
and someday I will be with him forever. The first

battle of our love might be over but the war to come is
going to be hell. Gabriela will not go down without a
fight and I fear what she might do to him.

I must leave and make sure Dean is safe, it's the only
way. If Gabriela knew that Dean loved me, she would
not rest until she took him from me.

I pull my phone out and shoot her a quick text, telling
her that she won't win this game. Dean is mine and
she can't have him and if she knew what was best for
her, she would back off.

I tell her that her secret of the accident would be
leaked to every newspaper in south Florida and that
she would be looking at murder chargers if she didn't
back off. Dad never knew why I wanted to work at
the pharmaceutical company and not one of his many
other places he owned. It wasn't the place I wanted to
work at to begin with but the testing and research
facility I grew up in was closed after the accident but
the data was stored at the new building. I told him
that I wanted to work in the archives room so that I
could find the proof I needed to bury Gabriela. All
the memory was erased from the hard drive but not all
the proof was gone. On my eighteenth birthday mom
had left me a surprise after her death. She had a
safety deposit box set up and I didn't know anything
about it until I turned 18. I wasn't sure what I was
going to find in it, but she left me directions to this

house and the location of the evidence that would convict Gabriela, if I so wanted too. I had to act fast and leave before Dean was caught in her web and couldn't be saved.

My phone rings, scaring me to death as I fumble to answer it. "Hello." I say quickly. The caller ID showed it was Bethany and I figured she had some information on Dean, but I didn't want to get my hopes up yet. "Hello." I say a few more times, trying to get her attention. Bethany is crying and there is a lot of noise in the background.

"Angelica. D-Dean is-." She's crying so much her words haven't come out. Something has her shaken to the core and I fear for what she must be seeing right now.

"Dean's what? What happened?"

"He's. He's. Angelica, he's."

"Dammit Bethany, spit it out!" I yell as my heart's racing and my hands are sweating. "What is it Bethany? Just fucking tell me already!" I yell at the top of my lungs. I want to know what is going on but whatever she is looking at has her messed up.

"Detective Moore found him tied to a chair." Oh, my God. Was he with someone? Were my worst fears confirmed?

"So, he was with a girl?" I say with hatred in my voice. I want to jump through the phone and kill him. I want to wrap my hands around his thick neck and squeeze until he turns blue in the face. I hate him. How could he do this? How could he just go and sleep with someone else right after me? What kind of guy was he? "I hate him! I hate him! I hope he dies!" I start yelling at the top of my lungs.

Bethany interrupts my rant.

"No, no he wasn't doing anything." Bethany's voice starts to shake as she tries to find a way to tell me the rest of what was going on.

"Then what dammit. What is it?"

"When he reached Dean, he was unconscious. Detective Moore found him tied to a chair and the house was on fire."

"OH my GOD!" Why did I say I hated him? Why did I wish he was dead? God. Why? Why would anyone do that to him?

"That's not the worst of it though, Angelica." I can't listen to what Bethany has to say. I feared that Dean was going to move on the moment I left him and I thought I was ok with that. My stomach is flipping right now as I think that I wished him dead just seconds ago and he might really be dead. Bethany hasn't told me if he is alive or not and I can't wait any longer to find out. I run to the bathroom and start throwing up. I want this nightmare to end and me to wake up back in bed with Dean. I want his strong arms wrapped around me one more time and his warm body pressed against me as we embrace each other. How do I go from that thought to the one I had earlier where I wished he was dead? He can't die. Dean is my protector and the one that was sent to help me. He was sent to end this war I have been fighting for so many years. He is my hero, riding a white horse, coming to my aid. "He had electrodes attached to his penis and he was being tortured for some reason. Detective Moore said that they were still on when he entered the house. He said Dean was unconscious due to the amount of pain he was in."

I can't believe what I'm hearing. I start crying as I try to stand and hold on to the sink. "Did you hear me, Angelica? Dean was being electrocuted. The sick bastards that did this to him, left him to die." Bethany is sobbing as she tries to tell me more, but I don't want to hear more, I can't.

"Bethany!" I yell to get her to shut up. "Is Dean ok? That's all I care about." I know she hated whoever did this to him as much as I do, but I must know if Dean is alive. Is he ok?

"Yes." She says after a few seconds.

"Good." I say as I try to control my breathing. I am shaking all over and I can't believe someone did this to him. Who would try to kill him? Gabriela? Gloria? Or, does he have more of a past I don't know about?

"Are you coming to see him?" Bethany breaks into my thoughts with a question that she should not have to ask but I hadn't even thought of. I'm still in shock. I look in the mirror at the teary eyed, scared little girl and I think back to ten years ago. I looked the same when I didn't want to see my mom die. I don't want to see Dean hurting or possibly dying but I must. I must leave and go to him.

"I'm leaving right now." I want to see him as soon as I can and I can't wait any longer.

"Please hurry, EMS is taking him to the hospital and he doesn't look good." Bethany's words hit me like a ton of bricks. He can't be hurt. I've seen him survive a car blowing up in front of him and he told me once a truck blew up while he was pulling a little girl from the wreckage. So, this should be nothing for him. Right? He must be ok. I love him.

Angelica

The drive was the longest eight hours of my life and it was hell on my brain. I ran everything through my head on what I would tell him when I laid eyes on him. I thought of how much of my past I would let him in on and how much of my future I will give him. But right now, I am ready to give him all he wants. Will he be the same person he was the other night? Will he still want to sweep me off my feet? Did he know that I brought this pain on him? Would he even forgive me once he found out the truth? I feel tears creeping up and I want to stay strong for Dean. He stayed strong for me. Detective Moore said it looked like whatever he was being tortured for, he never gave up any information. He also said that Dean woke up for a few seconds in the Ambulance and said to tell me he was sorry for everything and that my secret was safe. I don't know what he thinks he knows but I have more secrets than he can imagine.

How can I be worthy of a man that will lay down his life for a girl that broke his heart and ran off? I left Dean. I left him to die for me. What kind of person does that make me?

I reach the hospital and I'm ready for the worst. I am fully prepared for Dean to say that he never wants to see me again and to leave his life forever.

"Excuse me, ma'am? I am looking for Dean Mason, can you tell me where his room is?" The little old lady behind the counter types his name in the computer and then has a troubled look on her face.

"Give me one second sweetheart." She dials a number and then starts whispering something to someone but I can't make it out. "Someone will be down to help you in a second, honey." She smiles and motions for me to have a seat.

Is she calling security on me? Did Dean tell them not to let me come see him? Oh, God. Did he die while I was on my way? I pull my phone and check for any missed calls. There isn't any. I hear footsteps walking toward me and I see Detective Moore and what looks like a Doctor walking my way. My heart sinks to my stomach and everything goes black.

 "Angelica. Are you OK? Don't get up. Just wait." I'm not sure what happened but I am laying on the floor looking up at Detective Moore. Seeing the Doctor and him was more than I could take. "We need to talk to you."

"Where's Dean?"

"Dean's in a room sleeping. He is, well." My heart starts beating again and I'm finally able to breathe a little easier. I search both their faces. I know there's more. There is something they aren't telling me.

What else is wrong with Dean? Is he in a coma?

"What Detective Moore is trying to say is that Dean.
Well, he has some damage and issues with nerve
endings. Whoever electrocuted him, did a number on
his penis. It is scared and bruised. Once he wakes up
we will be able to tell if there is any permanent
damage." The doctor said my biggest fear yet, when
he wakes up. So, he is in a coma? My eyes fill with
water as I cover my face with my hands.

"It's all my fault, it's all my fault." I am sobbing and
repeating myself as they explain Dean is just knocked
out until they get a game plan on treatment in place.

"Angelica, remember the toxin your mom was
injected with before she died?" I never want to hear
that nasty word again. With everything else going on,
he wants to show off to some dick doctor about a drug
no one has heard of.

"What about it?" I snapped at him. He better have a
damn good reason for bringing that memory up
today?

"We found trace amounts of it in Dean's system.
Someone was poisoning him slowly with it. I don't
know if it was to kill him or use it to control him." I
can't remember a lot about the toxin, but
DexoLatrodectus is a powerful weapon if someone
knows how to use it. I hadn't heard any more about

the toxin since mom died.

"There is only one person that would know where the toxin was stored at. After mom got sick, the research team was able to get a neurotoxin made. I keep the formula on me always to remember mom by. She died before it could be finished though." I pull my phone out and show the Doctor what I'm talking about. I don't know why I keep it on my phone; I guess it's a way to never forget. I wish every day that the neurotoxin could have been completed before mom passed away but when your body is hit with a large dose like mom was, there is a window of opportunity that the neurotoxin can be used in. When you are injected with the toxin, your heart rate slows to one beat per minute or less. If CPR can be done for no more than 30 minutes and they receive the serum, the person might live. The theory is that the drug could be used to do high target assassinations and no matter if Emergency care is provided right away, it will take too long to discover the toxin is in the blood stream to safe them. But if the toxin is used over a long period, then it has a completely different effect on the body.

"Take her to see him now, we'll have this made in about an hour and get it rushed to him. If he was given too much, his heart would have stopped and no matter what we did, we wouldn't be able to save him." The doctor turns and walks down the long hallway to one of the research lab areas. As he walks off, I start thinking of mom lying in bed, her heart rate slowing as she squeezed my hand tight and smiled at me. She knew what was about to happen but she never lost her smile. As the toxin took hold of her, she never made a sound. She is the strongest person I know and she let her body relax as her heart suddenly stopped. The life that was keeping her with me floated away as I watched in horror my mother passing on. I never made a sound as she slipped away into a sleep that she would never wake from. It was hours later that I started to cry for her. I didn't want to face the fact that she was gone and if I never came to terms with that, then it would never be true.

"Come this way Angelica. He might not be awake yet, but we'll see." I am awakened from my thoughts and glad to see Detective Mooring leading me down a long hallway to some elevators. After a short ride, we are standing in front of Dean's room. I push the door to his room and a smell of smoke filled my lungs as I took in a deep gasp. Dean was lying there, not moving, just waiting for me. As I slowly step in the room, I notice the red, blue, green, yellow wires coming from every spot on his body. He had more wires on him than astronauts do when they get ready for space. "Oh, my GOD." I cry out as tears flow from my eyes. I want him to wake up where I can tell him I'm sorry. I want to tell him that I love him. I want to talk to him one last time. I didn't get to talk to mom in the last minutes of her life and I had left Dean in possibly the hours of his. I hold my face in my hand and weep.

Dean

After the house went up in flames I passed out.
Somehow, Detective Moore was able to unhook me
and cut the ties that were holding me to the chair. I
faintly remember hearing sirens and people yelling
but I don't remember being pulled from the house.
When I finally was able to taste fresh air, I kept telling
Detective Moore that I didn't tell them anything. I
told him to tell Angelica that I was sorry and that her
secret was safe with me. I was going to my grave
with where she ran off too. The main reason I didn't
tell them anything was because I didn't have a clue
where she was. I was going to spend the next day
looking for her and I thought I had a lead on where
she might have gone. After I talked to Bethany about
Angelica, I started thinking back to what she said
about her mom. Her mom got sick ten years ago and
her mom's friends died the day she got sick.

I started to realize that the day my parents died around
the same time her mom did. I'm pretty sure our
parents worked together at a research lab outside of
Pensacola. I hated that place and vowed never to
return, but I do remember the sweet little blonde girl
that I'm sure I fell for a long time ago. Mom and dad
never told me what they were working on but I read
reports that said they were creating a new weapon;
some type of mind control weapon. I wanted to check

the archive records at Mullers to see what I found out, but it's too late now to find anything out there. The weapon had potential to kill and that's what happened to my parents. One day when they were testing the weapon, a lab tech tried to steal some of the vials. When my parents tried to stop her, she injected them with the toxin and they died instantly. The image will be forever burned in memory of my mom and dad lying on the floor. The doctors told me their hearts just stopped. They thought it was a massive heart attack, but it wasn't. It was simple, the toxin blocked the neurons from firing in the heart and adrenalin from getting to the heart to pump. When I met Angelica, I didn't put two and two together. I realize now her mom was the head of the program and she was also injected with the poison. It was a lower dose, so it took a longer time to kill her, but it eventually did.

The night I took Angelica's virginity, I was going to tell her that she reminded me of someone. I wasn't sure who at first but now I know. I remember her blonde hair and her sweet face when I would go visit my parents. I can't believe I never realized it before now and I wonder if Angelica has known the whole time. She kept saying that she knew me but I thought she was thinking I reminded me of someone else. Why hasn't she said anything though?

The bright sunlight in the room is burning my eyes as

I try to open them. I hate the Florida sun right now and the brightness of the burning inferno. I hear someone crying and a males voice talking quietly to the person crying.

"Angelica?" I called out, hoping that someone had called her and she came to see me. I didn't want her here, she could still be in danger, but I'm glad if she did. She has been on my mind for the past few days and I can't wait to see her.

"I'm here Dean." Angelica's hand squeezes mine as I hear her sniff. She is trying to cover up her tears but she isn't doing a very good job at it. Every muscle in my body relaxes as she squeezes my hand tighter. I know she loves me and I love her.

"Why are you crying?" I say as I give her hand a little squeeze. I probably look like death warmed over laying in the bed but I still want to have fun with her.

"I'm not." She is a terrible liar but I love that she is trying to cover up some of her feelings for me. "Are you ok?"

"I was going to ask you the same question. I forgot to ask you the other morning when you left." She squeezes my hand tighter and laughs. She had no clue that I wanted to make sure I didn't hurt her the other night.

"I'm fine. Why would you ask that?" It's cute how clueless she is.

"I thought you might still be sore from the other night. I didn't want you hurting." I smile as she giggles. She slaps my arm and I feel a pain shoot through my body. *I'm definitely not dreaming.* I think as the pain slowly goes away. I guess she didn't want whoever is in the room to hear about her losing herself to me.

"What's wrong?" She snaps as she stands up searching my body.

"It's nothing. I just can't think of the other night too much. It still hurts." I forgot all about having my boys and big man shocked. It hurts to tighten up my penis, laugh or do anything, but seeing Angelica's smiling face makes me stir for another taste of her sweet wetness. Which makes it hurt even more.

"Oh, I forgot. Does it, um." Angelica bites down on her bottom lip and grins.

"I think it's fine. It's hard as a rock now that you are here, but it hurts. Damn, I'm going to have to think of your friend Detective Moore dancing in thong for me or something. I would take a cold shower if I could stand." I'm ready to have Angelica again and be buried in her deep all night long but I think I better wait a few days. Or longer.

"Good. And I don't think he will dance for you, but I can ask him." She smiles as she lays her head on my shoulder.

"NO!" I hear a male voice say from the corner of the room. "I'll give you some space. I'll be back a little later."

"Could have told me he was the other person in the room." I laugh as I play slap Angelica's hand out of the way. I don't care if he hears me or not, I need something to get her out of my head before I explode.

Detective Moore walks back into the room a few hours later, thankfully not dancing in a thong. I think I would puke at the sight of that. He has been giving Angelica and me some time together and I'm grateful. "The doc says you're going to make a full recovery."

"Yeah, everything still works and I have you to think for pulling me out of there in time. Why did you stop by in the first place though?" I'm not sure why he came by my house or how he knew where I lived but it seems a little odd.

"I called him." Angelica says as she sits up from a chair across the room. "I called him after I called Bethany. She said you quit your jobs and that you looked lost. So, I knew that whoever answered your phone wasn't just some one night stand slut. Which is what I thought she was at first."

"By the way, I would have beat the fucking shit out of you if I caught you with another woman." Detective Moore deadpans as he sits down in a chair next to Angelica. I don't think he's joking either. There is something between the two of them and he seems very protective of her.

"I knew something else had to be going on." She says as she shoots him a sideways glare. I forgot that the person who did this to me answered my phone.

"Speaking of that," Detective Moore adds. "Did you recognize who it was, Dean?"

"No," I say as I look down at my hands. "I wish I did. I heard their voices but I didn't recognize them. They were English. I think. But some of the words they said, made me think that they were from somewhere outside the US. I heard one say Nein once." Angelica interrupts me.

"That's German. Could it have been Gabriela?"

"I never thought of that. Maybe. The shadows would have been about the right height for her. But why would she want to kill me and why would she want information on Angelica? It makes no sense. I know you hate her as a step mom, but why would she want to know where you went to?"

"I told you she had a way to control you. She's

poisonous." Angelica pulls her knees up to her chest as she sits quite for a minute. I know she is upset and I don't know if she is upset with me or not.

"Do you mean she has the toxin?" Detective Moore asks Angelica.

I am lost. They are having a conversation about toxins and shit and I didn't know what the hell they were talking about.

"She doesn't, but her sister was the one that worked for my mom. Maybe she was the one that stole the vials that day. She must have been the one that killed your parents and my mom. Then they stole my dad by using the poison, to make sure no one would figure it out."

"I don't understand," I sit up in bed and turn to face them both. "Who is Gabriela's sister? Is she someone that we know? I remember reading the reports about someone else in the lab the day my parents died. But who was it?"

Angelica's face falls as if she just put the last piece of the puzzle together. I guess all this time she never knew who Gabriela's sister was. She knew that her sister worked in the lab with her mom, but she never knew her name.

Angelica

I never thought of it before now and for some reason it all makes perfect sense. She was the one that killed Dean's parents and my mom. She was trying to steal the toxin to give it to her sister. That's why Gabriela went after my dad. Dad was going to be the one to sell the toxin to different world powers because of his connections. They needed him to do their dirty work.

"Why did they need the toxin in the first place and why did they need your dad? I don't know how I play into this sick twisted game?" Dean's face is getting red and he is furious. He's thinking that he's been tricked by Gabriela and her sister and they were using him to get his parents old research. But they don't know who Dean really is. I've known from the first time I laid eyes on him but he didn't know who I was. I've always had a crush on him; when we were kids and now that we're both grown up. He looks so much better now. I knew Gabriela would try to steal him like she did my dad if she knew I liked him. That's why I called her and threatened her to leave Dean alone. It worked for a while, but he came running back to her on his own. She reminded me that she could kill him at any moment, and I knew she was capable of it. Each time she tried to hurt Dean it only made me want him that much more. He is perfect in so many ways. Nothing seems to shake him though and he never stops going for what he wants. Except the day he let me walk out of his life. I thought I could keep him safe and that I was doing the right thing by leaving but I know now he was trying to do the same thing.

"So are you telling me that Gabriela and her fucking sister killed my parents and you never told me?" Dean's voice grows louder and louder as he thinks about his parents dying. I never thought of telling him how his parents died when I first met him.

Roxanna told me that Dean was living in town and that I should go see him. She didn't know if he would recognize me or not but she said he was still suffering from the accident. She thought we could help each other but he never looked twice at me. Gabriela noticed me talking to him one morning and that's all it took for her to see if she could win him over. It didn't take much for him to be persuaded when she uses her poison for her own personal pleasure. I never knew that she was the reason my mom died or that her sister had worked so close to me for all this time. I knew Gabriela was poisonous and that she would not stop, until she had Dean, like she did my dad.

"That's not true Dean. I never knew that Gabriela did this with her sister. I didn't know she had anything to do with our parents dying. I thought she might have had the toxin and was using it on my dad but only found out she was using it on you when you came to the hospital."

"What do you mean, using it on me, and who the fuck is her sister?" Dean's voice is deep and stern now. He doesn't look at me with loving eyes. Hatred has replaced his soft hue.

"Gloria." I say as I shake my head. I thought Dean was following our conversation but I think we took an exit ramp and forgot to use a signal. He's lost. Dean's face goes pale and he closes his eyes while he processes everything. "The Doctor found trace amounts of the toxin in your blood. It wasn't enough to hurt you, but that might have been the reason you were so attracted to Gabriela and Gloria in the first place. Also, why were you attractive to me." I lower my head and feel guilt replacing our great night we spent together. I knew that once the Doctor told me about the toxin that was in Dean's blood, any woman that he found attractive, was increased by a hundred times. So much so, that he wouldn't be able to resist them at all. As the toxin wears off, he can make his own choices and think more clearly but I don't know if he chose me the night I lost my virginity, or if it was the toxin. I know I choose him of my own free will.

Dean

Mom once told me that I needed to make all decisions with my heart and to always listen to it. She said that sometimes things happen to good people and choices are made that will hurt others. She said to always search your heart and find happiness. That's why I waited for Angelica the day my parents died. I was going to tell her that I liked her and I wanted to hang out but fate had other plans for us.

I've been searching my heart to see if I can trust Angelica, or if she is using me to get my parents research material also?

"Dean, will please talk to me." Angelica looks up at me with her stunning blue eyes. They are filled with water and she has a hoarse voice. We had been arguing all night and this morning about stupid stuff from the past month. Most of the time the arguing would take place followed by an hour of sobbing. I hated that I had feelings of guilt and mistrust and I know she does too.

"I'm confused." I say with a sigh. I rub the back of my neck as I try to think of something better to say then just that. I want to believe everything she is telling and I want to know everything she remembers about the day of the accident. I also want to kill Gloria for what she did and it makes my stomach turn to think I thought I loved Gabriela at one time. How could I be so stupid?

"I know you are. I am too. But we can figure this out, together. I told Detective Moore everything and he is trying to locate Gloria and Gabriela now. Maybe we can get some answers soon." I know she's right and I know I shouldn't be so hard on her. She lost her mom and her dad was stolen from her. She had been threatened to stay away from me, but she came back. I know she loves me. I can see it in her eyes and I love her, but I'm afraid to tell her. I'm afraid that once those words are spoken aloud, my world will come crashing down on top of me. I know it's a three word phrase but it means so much. My favorite three word phrase growing up was, go fuck yourself, and it carries a lot of weight with it. If my mom ever heard me say that, she would have popped me in the mouth so hard, I would still be feeling it.

"The doctor said you can leave now if you want." A nurse proclaims as she comes into the room with papers for me to sign. I'm ready to leave and get the hell out of here. I'm not sure where I will go since my house burned to the ground.

"I still have a lot of questions. I'm sorry for fighting so much with you. Would you like to get a bite to eat? I want to know more about this toxin and figure out where we go from here." Angelica's face lights up

to the offer and she springs over to help me to my
feet.

"I can drive if you want." She offers as I sit down in
a wheel chair. I don't need one, but dumb policy says
that I must ride out of the hospital in one.

"Why do I need this chair?" I ask the nurse while
being pushed down the hall.

"It's policy sir. I'm sorry." The nurse says in an
annoyed tone. I guess she gets asked that all the time.

"I would like to know who owns this hospital and
give them a piece of my mind." I glance over to
Angelica, who hasn't been saying much, but now is
laughing at my last comment. "What the hell are you
laughing at?" I say as I slap her arm.

"My dad owns this hospital."

I start busting out laughing with Angelica and the
nurse stops dead in her tracks. I laugh even harder at
the expression on the nurse's face as she realizes she
was being rude earlier.

"It's ok. I don't talk to him much." Angelica tells the
nurse, trying to make her feel more at ease.

We make it out to the parking garage and Angelica
wants to take her car to get some food but I have a
better idea. Detective Moore arranged for my new car

to be delivered to the hospital the other day for me. I bought a new all-black 2020 Camaro SS.

"Camaro? Again?" Angelica grins at me. "After what happened to your last one, you think that's a good idea?"

I laugh and open the driver door for her to climb in. "Shut up and drive." I slam the door once she's in.

"Let's get something to eat, I'm starving." I tell Angelica as I slid in the passenger seat.

Angelica

Dean has a nice car and I know he is proud of what he has. He must have money saved up from the past years of working to buy the car out right. He said he didn't like payments, so he paid cash for the car. I know he works hard for his money and doesn't have millions in the bank like I do and I haven't told him I was rich. I never told him that my mom left me a ton of money when she died. He thought that since my dad kicked me out of his life, I had nothing anymore and I feel bad for not sharing that with him. Mom always said that I would know when the right man would show up in my life and love me for me and not for my money. She would be happy to know it's Dean. She always loved his parents and she knew him as well. After weeks of flirting, he was going to ask me something the day his parents died, but we never actually talked. I thought it was cute and I liked flirting but I was shy back then. He introduced himself and I will never forget his scared look on his face once the alarms went off. I never got a chance to tell him my name that day and I never had a chance either. Having your mom die in front of you makes you strong and tough fast and it changes people. For Dean, he didn't get to spend a few extra days with his mom before she died, instead, his whole world came crashing down on him in a few minutes. He was taken away and placed in foster care and I never knew where he was for the longest time.

We pull into a little restaurant that doesn't have many cars at it. We want some alone time to think and talk about our future.

As we push through the door, it opens to a little Greek restaurant with three other couples sitting at tables, waiting for their food to arrive. The inside of the restaurant looks like a little Greek town with marble tables and tile floors.

"Dean, I have a confession." The look on Dean's face held all the fear and terror of what he has been trying to hide for all this time. I don't know what he thought I was going to say, but he wasn't going to like what I was going to tell him. "I can't take your money." I look up at his eyes and see how blue they are with love. We weren't dating or anything and he did it because he cares for me, a lot.

"That money is a gift for you. It's to help you out." Dean reaches across the table and holds my hand. "I couldn't live knowing that you might have to go to some cheap hotel because you didn't have money to stay somewhere nice."

"But, I do have money." I hold his hands tighter as I prepare to tell him the truth about me. "My mom left me money. A lot of money."

The more I talked, the deeper blue his eyes turned for me. Dean is obvious to everyone else in the restaurant. The waitress has asked him three times for his drink order and I finally had to tell her to bring him water for now. He is hanging on to every word I am saying as he studies my face.

"I don't care if you have a million dollars or one dollar. I gave you the money so you could forget about your past and remember me." Dean's eyes fill with tears as he caresses my hand. "I know now that you and I are meant to be together."

"But Dean." I stop him before he can say anything else. I don't want to make this any harder than it already is. "I have a few millions in the bank and I don't want you to think that I didn't tell you cause you'd fall in love with my money and not me. I just. I don't know what I thought." My hands slip from his grip and down to my lap.

"Babe, I knew from the first time I laid eyes on you, that you were a heart throb. I knew you would be breaking hearts all over the place. I just never knew it was going to be my heart that you stole. I don't care how much money you have or don't have. I have money from when my…" My interrupts Dean before he can finish his sentence. I look down to see it's my dad calling. He never calls.

"Hello, dad? What? When? I'll be right there." My heart sinks in my chest and my knees go limp.

Dean

I can't believe what I'm hearing; Angelica is a
millionaire? I have about 500 thousand in the bank
and some small investments here and there, but she is
a freaking millionaire. It makes no difference to me,
but why would she want anything to do with me? I
don't have a job anymore and as far as she knows, I'm
broke. "Angelica, what is it?" The phone call she got
has her shaken. Her face turns red and flushed, then
her eyes become wide as she puts her phone down.

"My dad, he's. He's. Dead."

"Oh my God. What happened?" I jump to my feet
and wrap my arms around her. She is shaking all over
as she lays the phone down in her lap.

"They don't know. They found his car on fire and
there was a body in it. They think it's him. I have to
go see if I can identify him." I hold her tight as she
cries. I know she hates her dad with a passion but he
is still her dad. The news of his death came so quick
to her she is still trying to process the phone call.

"I'll drive you there. Where do we need to go?" I
pull her up in my arms from the chair and set her on
her feet. Together we walk toward the door hand and
hand. The doctor told me not to drive yet but I must
for Angelica. I haven't had pain meds in days and I

feel better since we left the hospital. We are almost at the car when I hear someone yell my name from behind us.

"What?" I call out as I turn around and notice no one is there. No one is around anywhere.

I turn to see if anyone is behind me, but no one is there. Angelica is already at the door of my car when I hear the door handle lift and then the sound of her body hitting the ground.

"Angelica? Angelica!" I yell as I run to her. She is laying on the ground next to the car and I lay my head on her chest, listening for her breathing and then I check for a pulse. I can't feel or see anything. I pull my phone out and dial 911. I hang up and start CPR right away. I know I need to get her to the hospital immediately. I don't know what happened to her but I know I'm not losing her.

"Breathe dammit, breathe." I pump her chest harder and harder as I curse out loud. "Just breathe." I can't believe what is happening. One second we are laughing and having fun and the next, this. It's my fault. It must be my fault. I have been doing CPR for fifteen minutes before the ambulance pulls up.

"Dean, whatcha got?" One of the medics asks as he comes running over to me from the truck. I'm not sure what to tell him. It was a crew that I knew when

I did my ride time and I kept in touch with some of
them to keep certified. "Dean, what is it?" I am
focused on doing CPR and I don't turn to look at him
as he asks me a few times what happened. "DEAN!"
He grabs my shoulders and shakes me as hard as he
can to get my attention. "What the FUCK
happened?"

"I... I don't know. I'm not sure. I found her like this.
I found her not breathing, so I started CPR. I don't
know what happened." The medic hooks her lifeless
body up to a monitor and tells me to stop what I am
doing. Three straight lines go across the screen
showing Asystole rhythm.

"I'm sorry Dean, but she's gone."

"Shut up, she's not dead. No. She's not dead." I
keep yelling louder and louder as I start CPR again.
The medic reaches down to stop me from doing CPR.

"Dean. She's gone. There's nothing we can do." He
repeats as I turn and knock him in his mouth as hard
as I can. Blood gushes everywhere. She isn't going
to die. I'm not going to allow it.

"No she isn't. She can't be. I love her. I know now
that I love her."

"Let's call it." The medic looks down at his watch
and starts to open his mouth.

"NO. Fuck NO. I want to keep working her to the hospital. She can't be gone." The medic tries to fight with me again and I pull my arm back to knock him out this time. I will load her in the ambulance myself and take her if I have too.

"Load her up and let's go." A deep rumble comes from behind me. It's Jay, we call him the Paragod. A term given to medics that KNOW they are the shit. He was and still is a mentor to me. "You heard me. Let's go."

We load her limp body on a stretcher and head toward the hospital.

I know I must keep her heart beating and keep breathing for her and I am going to let her die. I love her. I didn't get a chance to tell her. But I love her.

"Faster dammit. Can't we go faster?" I yell at Jay in the back of the Ambulance as my hands are still on her chest doing compressions. I am ready to move anyone that stands in my way of getting Angelica to the hospital. I don't want to look at her face as I pump her chest. I can't look. I must focus on what I'm doing and block everything else out. I have a spot between her breasts picked out and I'm working as hard as I can to keep her blood pumping. I can't lose her. I can't.

"I'm going to shock her, Dean. Move back." Jay

pushes a button on a machine that has wires going to her chest. He makes sure I'm not touching her as the shock is delivered to her body. That's all he needs right now is for me to not listen to him and touch her while he shocks her. I have seen people hold on to loved ones when a crew shocks the patient and the conscious person is now a patient as well. "Clear." He yells as her body jumps from the shock. Jay pulls out a big needle and fills it up with epi. "Stand Back." Jay plunges the needle down into her chest, going into her heart.

"Dean, did you check her sugar?" Jay asks as he lifts one of Angelica's hands up.

"No, why?"

"Look at her finger tip. She has a needle mark. Maybe she was."

"FUCK!" I scream at the top of my lungs. I know what it is, I know exactly what happened. That fucking bitch tried to kill me and Angelica. "Call the hospital and tell them that we are bringing in a nineteen-year-old that has been injected with DexoLatrodectus. The hospital's working on a neurotoxin. We have to keep her heart pumping until we get there." Jay reaches over and grabs the mic to tell the hospital everything I just told him. He also says that we are bringing in family. Even though Jay didn't know Angelica, him and I go way back and he wants to make sure the hospital treats her like family.

"Hold on guys, were almost there." The driver yells back to Jay and me.

"How could I have been so stupid? How did I not see this coming?" I'm still talking to the lifeless body that is in front of me. CPR is hitting twenty-minutes now and I don't know what else to do. I know Angelica said there was a thirty-minute window before the toxin would kill someone because the heart isn't completely stopped. I don't understand all about the toxin and hope to never have to deal with it again after today.

As we pull into the hospital Jay helps me unload Angelica's body on a hospital stretcher that is waiting on us.

"We've got her guys." A doctor injects her with the neurotoxins as they rush her through the doors into the ER. A couple security officers stop me at the door and won't let me follow her in.

"Move out of my fucking way!" I yell at them. I'm ready to go through anyone at this point and no one is going to stop me. They stay firm at the door and won't let me pass. I know they are doing their jobs but why won't they let me in? "I'm warning you." I threatened one last time. Neither of them budge though. "Fine, have it your way." I pull my arm back, ready for a war with these clowns.

"Dean." I feel Jay wrap his large arms around my body and hold me tight. "Calm down Dean. Let the Doctors do their job. Calm down." I know he's right, but I don't care. I want to hurt someone for this. I don't care who.

"Keep that crazy bastard under control." The other medic yells at Jay as I finally calming down and the adrenaline is wearing off.

"Are you good Dean?" I give him a node and sink to the ground. My energy is spent and I don't feel like fighting anymore. "Stay calm Dean, she'll be ok." Jay's words are what I need to hear as I slow my breathing down and try to reassure myself that I got Angelica here with enough time to spare.

"He's fucking crazy, Jay. He punched me for no reason." The other medic is still pooping off at the mouth as I shake my head and close my eyes. If I had any energy left, I would close his mouth for him.

"I told you when we pulled up, Angelica is family. She is one of us. I've known her for a long time and I have known Richard for a long time. We take care of our family. We don't half ass shit in the field when it comes to family." Jay's voice keeps getting louder and louder as he walks toward the medic. "And we sure to hell don't stand in the way of someone trying to save our family." Jay's big fist bust the little prick in the mouth. You can hear his jaw shatter as blood spews out of his lips. "NOW, SHUT, THE FUCK, UP!" I laugh as I see him fall to the ground as a mountain of a man stands over him to see if he says another word about his family. Jay acts as though Angelica is a little sister and he will do anything to protect her.

Dean

"Dean. You can see her now if you wish." Do I want to see her? Do I want to accept this fate? Why? Why? It was my car, not hers. They were after me, not her.

"We got'em, Dean. It's over." Detective Moore comes walking in with a file in his hand.

"Is that the people that were trying to kill me?" I ask, pointing at the file. I want to know who they are, I just want to find out who hurt her. I want to know who tried to kill me and who did this to Angelica? Was it Gabriela? "I want to kill them." I turn to Detective Moore clenching my fist as I grind my teeth. "I want them to pay for this."

"They will Dean. They will." He tries to reassure me, but it isn't working. "Have you seen her anymore?"

"No, I can't take it anymore. I had to walk away. How could she be?" I can't finish my sentence. The pit of my stomach is turning as I think of Angelica and what has happened to her. How could anyone do something this mean to a sweet, innocent girl like her. My heart begins to race as I think of her laying there. "So, Gabriela and Gloria isn't the ones behind this?"

Detective Moore takes a deep breath and lets it out

slowly. "Maybe. We still don't know where they are. These two women came forward and turned themselves in this morning and they admitted to killing Nicholas and to trying to kill you. They also said that Angelica was not a target, but they were glad of what happened to her."

I can't believe it; Gabriela and Gloria are going to make a clean getaway. "So, what happens now?" I ask Detective Moore.

"Let's go see her. Then we'll talk about it."

The hallway is dark and the whole floor has been moved out. I'm not sure if I can go in and do this, but I must. I must see her, no matter how much I don't want to.

I push the door open slowly and I can hear Bethany standing next to the bed crying. No. I can't. I want to turn and run, but I need to see her. I tried so hard to get her here with enough time.

I clear my throat as I walk slowly into the room. Bethany turns and smiles at me as I move quietly across the tile flooring.

"She's beautiful." Bethany says with tears running down her face. I close my eyes and turn my head as I bite the inside of my low lip to fight off crying.

I bite as hard as I can into my lip but it doesn't stop

the tears from coming. They slowly make their way out of my eyes and down my cheeks. They sting my lips as they fall to the ground.

"Why are you crying?" Angelica lifts her head up a little off the pillow and looks at me.

"Are you ok?" I lean down close to her face and kiss her lips softly. I don't want to make her move too much.

"I am fine. I was told that you broke someone's nose to get me here." She grins and winces because of the pain from the surgery.

"Jay broke the guy's jaw afterwards, so it wasn't just me." I say grinning. "I wanted to break every bone in his body for telling me you were dead." I reach for her hand to hold it tight. "I guess you heard about your *dad*, that someone did identify the body?" I know Bethany had explained to her what happened already but I was just making sure she didn't leave anything out.

"Yeah, my new sister told me." She looks up at Bethany and grins while saying it.

"What?" I jerk my head around to look at Bethany, who has a big grin on her face.

"Turns out my dad knocked up a girl before meeting mom, and Bethany was their kid. When his Will was read, he left everything to me and her. The attorney said that the Will was just changed a couple weeks ago. Gabriela doesn't get a thing." I can't believe it. Angelica might have lost a father but she gained a sister. How weird.

"*I'm screwed.*" I whisper under gritted teeth. "Um. I need to tell you something about Bethany." I look down at the floor and try to think of the best way to explain to her that I slept with her. I kind of figured she already knew, but I never came out and told her. Well, I didn't sleep with her. I fucked her, real hard and then tossed her aside and never called her again.

"Bethany told me everything. Don't worry about it." I feel a hand touch my face and I look down to see Angelica smiling at me. "I love you."

"I love you too."

"I know. Or you wouldn't have fought so hard to help me."

Angelica

Dean stayed with me in the hospital and never left my side once. I was starting to get annoyed with him constantly wanting to do everything for me. He wouldn't let me lift a finger and I know he loves me, but damn. It's been nice talking to Bethany about my dad though. She has his eyes but it's sad that she never knew him other than what the papers would write about him. I feel sorry for her. It must be hard not knowing who your father was. Dean still acts nervous around Bethany and it's kind of funny. I didn't get the details of what happened the night they had sex, but by the way Dean is acting, it must have been intense. Bethany assures me that it was a one night thing and that's it. I trust her and I trust Dean, now. He was drugged before and he did a lot of things that he regrets. Since he has been with me he hasn't looked at another woman. I can tell how much he has changed since the toxin neutralized.

"Angelica." Detective Moore says as he walks into the room. "We've found some information about Gabriela and Gloria."

"What is it?" I ask.

"Turns out that both of them didn't run like we thought. They are still here somewhere in Orlando. I don't think it's safe for you or Dean to stay here any longer."

"Where will we go?" Dean's voice was shaky as he asked.

"I know a spot." I didn't tell Dean about the house my mom left for me and I know it will be a shock to him.

Being discharged from the hospital was an easy process. Since I own the hospital now, all the nurses were extremely nice to me and were falling over each other to make sure I had everything I wanted. We made our way down to Dean's car and I didn't want to touch anything on it.

"Don't worry, it's been cleaned by the police. Nothing is going to hurt you. I promise." Dean's voice makes me feel better, but he can't promise me something like that. There is no way to know if something will ever hurt me again. I do know one thing about him though, he isn't going to let anything get to me again if he can stop it. I know he loves me and that he will protect me forever, but I didn't realize how much he loves me.

"So, where's this place that you want to go?" Dean asks as we pull out of the parking garage.

Dean still doesn't know about the house and I guess I better tell him now before he sees it and flips out.

"It's at Sapphire Coast, close to Pensacola." I say as I try to get comfortable in the passenger seat.

"Sounds perfect. I love the water." Dean never asked anymore about the house or where we were going to live. He was just happy with whatever made me happy.

"Bethany is going to come live with us as well. She's my sister and I want to get to know her." I wasn't asking for his permission if she could or not live with us. I am telling him that she is going to live with us, whether he likes it or not. So, he needs to man up and deal with it.

I can see the hesitation in his eyes as he processes what I just told him.

"Whatever makes you happy, baby." He finally says.

Dean

Angelica slept most of the way to Sapphire Coast and I don't blame her. She gave me directions on how to get there and I told her to take a nap and not worry about me. I can't believe she was so close to dying and I made a deal with God. If he saved her, I would marry her one day. I just hope she says yes. As we pull up to the address she gave me, I see a large stone house that sits right on the beach. The house is three stories with a large porch around back. Angelica said that it was a small house that her mom had left for her, but this isn't a small house. My old house could fit inside this one, twice over, before it burned to the ground.

"Sweetheart, I think we are here." Angelica stirs and opens her eyes to the gorgeous gulf sun.

"I hope you like it." She smiles and takes my hand.

"Like it? I love it." I can't believe this is going to be our new home. We can put the past behind us and make a new life together. The only problem is Bethany. Angelica insisted that Bethany came with us and she made a great argument on why she should come. She thought Gloria or Gabriela would try to hurt her if they found out she was Nicholas's daughter. After looking at the house, I realized why Angelica said we would have enough room for her to stay with us. Maybe I could move past being such a dick to her and accept her as Angelica's new sister and not a piece of ass I tossed aside.

As we walk into the large open living room Angelica wraps her arms around me.

"I've waited long enough for this." She press's her soft lips against mine and slowly slips her tongue into my wanting mouth.

"Calm down, the Doctor said to take it easy." I remind her as I catch my breath. I have been waiting for days to do the same thing to her, but I thought it would be best if we took it slow for a few days. Angelica didn't have the same idea as I did though.

"The hell with that. I wanted you before you saved my life. Now, I want my hero even more." She wraps her arms around my neck and I lift her off the ground with ease. I run my hands up her back, lifting her shirt as I go. She raises her arms as the shirt slides off her perfect body. She isn't wearing a bra and the scar from her recent surgery is still prominent on her chest. I don't want to be forceful with her and hurt her in any way. I slowly lift her higher as my mouth finds her nipple and my tongue draws circles around it. Her hands are pulling at my head and my hair as she moans. I know I should stop but it feels so damn good. The more she moans the more I want to be inside her again.

"Take me. Please." She cries out as I start to lower her down. I was planning on sitting her back on the ground and waiting for a few days before I made love to her, but her cries made me ready to explode. I carry her over to a leather couch and lay her bare back down as I slowly kiss her neck. I pull her shorts and panties off her and she lets out a squeal as her naked ass hits the cold leather. I softly kiss her scar on her chest and make my way down to her flat stomach. She still has a hand full of my hair as she throws her head back, letting a moan fill the space between us. My hand opens her legs and my fingers traced a spot up to her wetness.

My fingers slid across her as my thumb separates her folds. Her body kisses my thumb as I press past them, etching deeper into her. A small scream comes from her as her hips shift under the pleasure.

"Oh, I've missed this." I confess as I long for more.

"Me. Too." Her head arches back as her breathing increases. She is already close to coming and I haven't got to taste her yet. She moans and screams as my lips wrap around her as I inhale her intoxicating scent and pull her into my mouth.

"I'm going to come. OH! I'm going to come!" She screams louder as my tongue enters deep into her body and my thumb rubs her. It's been over a week since she lost her virginity and she is ready to lose herself to me again.

"Come for me. Come for me, baby." A burst of energy hits her body and she moans louder as the organism consumes her. She pulls my hair and screams as she rocks against my mouth.

"Holy shit, motherfucking good Lord." She exhales as her built up tension is released. I have heard Angelica let out some words before but she was not holding anything back today when she came.

"We're not done yet." I pull my shirt and pants off as she lays on the couch still trying to catch her breath. I know she is thinking that I am going to kill her with how large she has just made me but I plan on taking it slow with her.

"I'm ready for you. Don't hold back Dean. Please, don't hold back." Angelica closes her eyes as she prepares for me to enter her. I know I should wait and give her body more time to heal before I pound her with the force I want to. But if I go slow and take my time, I can control the amount of pressure I put on her.

I slowly push inside her as she shifts her hips, ready for me. "Oh, fuck." I cry out from the pain of her hand wrapped around me as I push deeper. I am still sore from where I was electrocuted but I don't care.

"Harder, Dean. Harder." I am not holding anything back unlike the night when she lost her virginity. Her moans become more and more intense as she rubs herself faster. For someone that has never had sex but one time in their life, she knows what do with her hands and how to tighten her body to drive me crazy.

"Come for me baby. Come." I whisper as her body begins to tremble with pleasure. I thrust a few more times as she tightens down on me. A smile shines across her face as she pulls her middle finger up to her mouth and sucks her wet finger. "Holy shit." I scream as she giggles at the pulse that is sent through my body. "Aw."

We both lay on the couch with her legs wrapped around me as I stay deep inside her. We don't care that we're naked in the living room with all the windows open for the world to see us. We are wrapped around each other in a state of ecstasy as our scent is now that of sex.

Angelica

"Dean?" My legs are sore and my body aches all over from our fun we just had. We had a full night of passion and Dean made love to me at least five times. He made me come so many times that I passed out. The Doctor warned me not to overdo anything, but how can I resist Dean Mason. He is gentle and took it slow, making sure he didn't hurt me during our night of pleasure.

"Dean?" I don't see him anywhere in the room as the sun shines brightly from the windows from the far wall. I guess I overslept but it doesn't matter. We don't have to work if we don't want to for the rest of our lives. If I have Dean, I will be happy. "Dean? Where the hell are you?"

"In here." Dean calls out from the kitchen. He's fixing breakfast for me and already has a plate waiting on me at the bar. I smell the most heavenly smell ever, Bacon. "Thought you could use some energy after last night." As I sit down at the bar he leans over and holds my chin as he presses his lips to mine. "This will never get old."

"Last night will." My face turns red as Bethany walks up and sits down next to me at the bar. "Damn, how many times did you do it last night? Geez." Bethany is laughing as she slaps my arm. "Your doctor said to take it easy, I'd hate to see you two when you're not taking it easy."

"Sorry Bethany, I forgot you were going to be staying here. I. I just. Needed Dean." I smile as I take a drink of orange juice.

"It's cool sis. Just warn me next time." Sis? I never thought that I would have a sister, but now that I do, she thinks I am a slut. I bury my head down into my hands. I've never had family, except for Roxanna. After mom died, something died in me too. I tried to date and I even had a boyfriend, but it didn't seem right. Now I have a man that loves me and a sister that I need to get to know, and now she sees me as a slut on our first day together.

"How's the food?" Dean's sexy voice steals my thoughts.

"It's good. Where did you learn how to cook?" I say looking up from hands.

"It's bacon and eggs. It's not that hard." Dean laughs. I guess for him it isn't that hard but I can screw up toast.

Dean is perfect and he didn't mind waiting on Bethany and me as we set and talked. After we finished eating, Dean started cleaning the dishes and never seemed to mind at all.

"Thank you, Dean." I say as I wrap my arms around his neck.

"For what?"

"Everything." I kiss his lips and squeeze his neck tight as I roll on the ball of my feet. I am wearing one of Dean's shirts and the more I raise my arms the more my butt shows from under it. Dean places his hands on my bare ass and picks me up on the counter. I'm nothing for him to lift and throw around anyway he wants too. His waist is lined up between my legs as he presses forward. I can feel him poking me as he leans forward more.

"No panties? You're a bad girl." His tongue hits mine and my stomach flutters as he pulls me in closer to his hard chest.

"Well... I'm going to the other room." Bethany says from behind Dean. I forgot about her even being in the same room with us. I give her a wave as Dean tears his shirt from my body.

"Oh God." I scream as shockwaves shoot through my body. I can't wait any longer for him to take me. I pull Dean's shorts down and he springs up, ready for me. I am very sore from last night but I want more. He thrust deep into me as I scream out in pain and pleasure. The screams echo through the kitchen and Dean moans as I kiss his neck and claw at his back.

"I'm going outside." Bethany proclaims from the other room loudly. I don't care where she goes; I want Dean in me and I don't care who is around.

Bethany

It has been nice living in a beach house with nothing to do but watch the waves roll in. I love it here and I love that I have a sister. My mom gave me up for adoption when I was one year old and I lived in foster care for years. When I was fifteen I headed out on my own. I got a few jobs here and there to keep an apartment in Orlando. Rent isn't cheap at all. I never had anything or anyone in my life to look up too. I met Dean one night and we had one night of passion, but nothing like he shows Angelica now. I can see that he loves her. I know it must be hard for Angelica to think that I also fucked Dean, but he was a different person then and I can see the way he looks at her and he never looked at me like that.

"Bethany, want to join us?" Angelica yells at me from across the house. Her and Dean were dressed and heading somewhere. I don't know where, but anywhere to get out of the house sounds good to me. It's been a while since I've seen the outside world.

"Where are you going?" I ask, like it matters.

"There's an ambulance service here that we own, let's go check it out. Maybe we can do some work, just so we don't go stir crazy." Now that sounds like the best plan anyone has had yet. I'm still getting used to the idea that we own different businesses and that I have money in the bank. I'm not sure what I'm supposed to do but I figure Angelica will help me along the way.

Dean pulls up to a large building that has three bay doors on it. Each door is open and we can see about ten ambulances inside. They are nice. This isn't a poor town and the ambulance service here makes money.

"What are we going to tell them? We own you now and we all want to work here?" I ask Dean and Angelica.

"I called the director and told him that we were coming and that we own the company, now that our dad passed away. So, let's just see how things go." Angelica has a plan and she seems like she knows how to run a business.

"You must be Angelica, I'm Dave." A tall, dark-haired man says as he walks up to all three of us. He is checking each of us out, but mainly focuses his attention on Angelica. Of course, she is the one with brains and natural beauty.

"Hi, Dave. This is Dean and my sister Bethany." Why didn't she introduce Dean as her boyfriend or anything like that? Last I knew they were dating.

After we talk for a little while in the front office, Dave

shows us around the building. Then he takes us to meet the crews that are working for the day. Everyone is stretched out on a couch in a large break room that has a game playing on the TV. It looks so relaxing.

I scan the room, looking at everyone and taking in all the new faces.

Oh, my. My heart stops beating, and I swallow hard to make sure I'm not dreaming. Sitting on the couch are two of the hottest guys I have ever seen. Both look like models and they have large arms and thick necks. Their chests are about to bust out of the shirts they are wearing. Both have longer hair that is dark, and both have the darkest brown eyes I have ever seen. They are sexy. Damn are they sexy. I feel myself get wet as I start to throb between my legs. I want to know how they would feel inside, at the same time. I bit my bottom lip and suck in a breath. Oh, God, I want them right now while everyone watches.

"Hi, I'm Adam and this is my brother Aaron." Did he just say brother? My panties are soaked and my legs grow weaker. They must be twins and I want to know if they both look the same everywhere.

"Bethany, they're talking to you." I hear Angelica's voice say from behind me. I still can't move. I'm frozen by their stare. "Bethany." Angelica hits me in the back to wake me up from my day dream of fucking them both.

"Oh, sorry. Hi. My name is Bethany." I manage to get out without sounding like a complete idiot.

"Nice to meet you, Bethany." Both brothers are standing in front of me and I can't picture anything more than taking them right there.

Out of nowhere a loud noise comes over the speakers and the two brothers look at each other and then back at me. "I'm sorry, Bethany. We have to make a run. We hope to see you again soon." Both say as they finish each other's sentences as they talk. They push past where I'm standing and one brushes my arm as he walks by.

"I want you." I say as his touch about sets me off.

"Excuse me?" Adam turns and looks at me grinning. "I didn't hear what you said." Oh, my God, did I say that out loud?

I drop my head and shake it to tell him I didn't say anything, but they heard what I said. My face is turning red and I can feel the heat rising through my body.

"I hope to see you when we get back. If that's ok?" He says as he walks out of the break room. I watch his ass in the tight pants he is wearing and I want to take him right now. Him and his brother.

"Bethany, you ok?" Dean is looking at me funny and I realize my breathing has increased and my face feels hot. Damn, I'm a fucking mess.

"I'm fine. I. I'm just."

"You're just horny. That's what you are." Angelica says as she walks out of the room laughing.

Damn, was I that obvious.

Dean

After talking with Dave for a little while, he agreed there was a spot for me on one of the trucks. Angelica said I didn't have to work any if I didn't want to but I wanted to do a little bit of work to keep busy. I really didn't care anything about working but she insisted on working there a few days out of the week and I wanted to keep an eye on her. Mainly because I didn't like the way Dave looked at her when we first met him. He's creepy. He's tall, about my height, but he's not as big as I am. He has dark hair and dark eyes. There is something about the way he grinned at her that made me want to punch him in his face. I don't know what it was but I don't trust him. Since I don't trust him, I don't plan on leaving her side for a while. She also didn't introduce me as her boyfriend to him and that kind of pissed me off. After everything we've gone through, she just said, this is Dean and nothing more.

"Angelica, why are you going to work at the ambulance service? I don't like the idea of you working there. What if something happens to you?" I know I am being over protective, but I almost lost her and I'm not going to lose her again.

"I can't stay here all day and do nothing. Don't worry about me."

"But I do. I also worry about you being around Dave. I don't trust him." I know I'm being jealous, and very overprotective now, but who gives a shit, that's what I'm supposed to do.

"What the hell's your problem? Dave seems like a nice guy." Angelica snarls at me.

"Is that why you didn't introduce me as your boyfriend to him?"

"No, you fucking jerk. I didn't interduce you as my boyfriend because you never asked me out, dumb ass. And did you ever stop and think that maybe I get jealous knowing that you fucked Bethany, which is prettier than me and is filled out more? Every time she walks into the room, you try to not stare at her. I don't know if it's because you want to bend her over the counter and fuck her while her tits bounce up and down or if you're embarrassed. Maybe you think you can live out some sick fantasy and fuck us both and we can be sister wives for you. You're such a fucking jerk. You fucking hypocrite." Angelica slams the bedroom door and leaves me standing in the hallway with a dumb expression on my face. I have never heard her use the F word so many times before and I know she is mad at me.

She has every right to be mad at me too. I'm a dumb ass. A fucking dumb ass.

"Where you going?" Bethany asks as I walk out the front door toward my car. She had been sitting there the whole time listening to everything that we were saying. I try not to look at her because I am embarrassed about the way I treated her not because I think of having sex with her. Bethany is a nice girl and she shouldn't have been used by me because I had a bad day.

Angelica

I hear the front door close and Dean's car start up. His new Camaro has a loud exhaust that echoes through the empty house, making me cringe as he floors it out of the driveway. I didn't mean to go off on him and I didn't even realize that I didn't mention him as a boyfriend to Dave. I've been all over the place with my emotions lately and I don't know what's wrong with me. I think of Dean as more than just a boyfriend. He's my hero. He saved me when I needed help and he's always been there to help me. How could I have been so dumb? How?

A quick knock at the door breaks my thought.

"Angelica, can we talk?" Bethany peeks her head in through the door. "I didn't know you felt that way about me. If I did, I would've never come with you guys. I'm so sorry. What Dean and I had wasn't love. You two have that. I see it in his eyes. He loves you and only you. I'll pack my things up and move out. Again, I'm so sorry." I try to hold back even more tears, but Bethany was right. Dean did love me and I yelled at him and pushed him away, again.

"I love him. I hate that I can't trust him though. Why can't I trust him?" My tears won't hold back anymore and once again I'm a crying mess.

"Because of your dad." I loved my dad but he loved Gabriela more than his daughter and his wife. I never forgave him for running off and I thought that when he reached out to find me, it was to put the pieces back together. I never thought it was just to try to steal mom's work from me.

"Where did Dean go?"

"I don't know. He didn't say anything as he walked out. I'm sure he will be back. I'm sure of it." Bethany's words did little to comfort me. She starts to stand and walk away to go gather her things.

"Where are you going?" I ask her through my sobs. I know I'm jealous of her and a part of me hates her for being so pretty, but another part of me loves her. She's my sister now and the only family I have left.

"I told you, I'm packing my things and am leaving." Bethany's trying to make our new relationship work and she doesn't want to do anything to mess up the bond that sisters should have.

"I don't want you to leave. I'm sorry for feeling jealous and saying those things about you. I had no right to say that about you. I probably will feel this way for a while but please don't leave. You are the only family I have." Bethany runs over and hugs me. Both of us are crying now. I want her to stay with me and I want her to be my sister. I also want her to feel comfortable around Dean and me. When he comes back, we all are going to have a long talk.

I wake up to an alarm clock going off next to the bed but I don't remember setting one. I stayed up late waiting for Dean to come home, but he never did. Maybe I ran him off for good this time. Bethany and I stayed up a while talking and she told me the whole story of how her and Dean met and what happened. I understand now why Dean doesn't want to look at her sometimes and is nervous around her. He was dick and treated her like an even bigger dick. How could I be so stupid? He loves me so much and I pushed him away.

"Dean," I call out hoping it was him that set the alarm when he got home. Maybe he came back when I was sleeping but where is he now? I tried calling him last night but his phone would ring and ring. Bethany said she heard it ringing on the bar; I guess he left it and didn't want to be bothered by me anymore. I can't blame him.

"Dean, baby? Are you here?" I keep praying that I will hear his deep voice and he will step out of the shadows and take me in his arms.

I reach the alarm clock and turn off `` Love is Your Name by Steven Tyler. I told Dean I liked that song the other day while we were driving and I wonder if he set my alarm to play it?

"What the hell is that?" A piece of paper is sitting next to the alarm clock and I recognize Dean's scribble, it's not hard to pick it out anywhere.

Angelica,

I know I haven't been perfect and you're more than I deserve. I'm sorry for running off last night and not letting you know where I went. I would love to be your boyfriend, if the job is still open. But I would love to be with you forever as well. I love you with my heart.

Dean

Ps Follow the roses.

I brush a tear away from my eyes as I look out the bedroom door and see a line of pink and red roses. *What are you up to Dean?* I think to myself. The roses go from the bedroom, to the back porch and then from the back porch to the sand. When my bare feet hit the sand, a sensation shoots through my body. The air is moist and cool from the morning tide. I'm wearing one of Dean's shirts and nothing else. It comforted me last night when I thought he was gone. I follow the roses down the beach and I can see a figure standing by the water's edge. The sun is just coming up and I can't make out who it is yet.

Marry Me by Train starts playing softly as I walk toward the figure. The sun is slowly coming up and I can see Dean, standing in a black suit with his arms around his back. As I step closer the music fades away to a whisper in my ear as the Gulf breeze blows my hair back. My heart is racing and I suck in a breath as Dean kneels to one knee.

"Angelica Muller, will you make me the happiest man alive?" My heart is going a thousand times a minute. I can't feel my legs because of the excitement. The cool air is taking my breath away as I try to remember how to breathe. "Will you Marry Me?" My eyes swell with tears and I suck in an even deeper breath with my hands covering my mouth.

"Yes, yes. God, yes." I throw my arms around

Dean's neck, nearly knocking both of us into the water. "I will Dean. I will. I love you." My face is stinging with tears as I kiss Dean. I love him so much. I always have. He didn't run off last night. He was planning this. I thought that he left and never wanted to speak to me again.

"I love you, Angelica." I melt in his arms and he slips the diamond ring on my left hand.

"It's gorgeous." I choke through tears. I can't breathe. All my wishes are coming true. Dean swoops me in his arms and carries me back to the house. Bethany is crying at the door when I show her the ring. He wouldn't let me stop to show her it up close. He had a wild look in his eye and he wasn't stopping until my back was flat on the bed.

Angelica

It's been nice not having to worry about going to
work every day and I think I could get used to
relaxing on the beach and live off my dad's money for
the rest of my life. Dave called and said he had a job
for all three of us at the ambulance service if we
wanted it. I think it's funny that he offered us a job.
When I told him that we wanted to work there for a
few days, I wasn't asking him for permission, but I
guess he doesn't want to take orders from a 19 year
old. He told Dean the other day he could work there
but never told him when he could start. It's nice
though that all three of us will be going to work
together, even though Dean will be doing the hardest
part of the job. He is going to work on the truck for a
few weeks to see how the crews work together and get
a feel for how everything runs. I am going to do
paperwork and Bethany, she is going to do what she
does best, flirt.

"If you need anything today just call me." Dean says
as he heads out to the bay to check his truck. He has a
bad feeling about Dave and made me promise to tell
him if he tries anything.

"Stop worrying. I have my own office and a ton of
stuff to do. I'll be fine." I give him a kiss and tell
him to have a great day. I want to see where the
service stands with the yearly budget and get a jump

on next year's budget. There are also personal files I
need to look through. I want to see who is working
for us. I haven't felt the best for about a week now
and I am tired for some odd reason. I am ready for
the new challenge. Dean, Bethany and I finally had a
long talk about how much of dick Dean was and now
they are getting along better. I know it's hard for both
of them and I don't blame Dean for his actions. I
knew he liked to have fun and I remember what
Roxanna told me about him but I never knew it was
from the toxin. She told me the other day how much
he seems like he's calmed down. I was so excited to
tell her I was engaged. She was supposed to be back
in Orlando last month but didn't make it. I've talked
to her a few times on the phone and I hope she can
make it to the wedding.

"Fine, but can we at least have lunch together? Let's
say around noon?" Dean is not going to be happy
unless I agree to his demands so I give in.

"Fine, noon it is. Love you. Now go to work before I
have to fire you." I slap his ass as he starts to walk
away.

"Keep that up and we will be trying out your new
desk." I gasp for air and shake my head. It's our first
day at work and we can't get caught doing it on my
desk. Not the first day at least.

"Go to work." I snap at him, trying not to think of

how wonderful he would feel buried deep inside me.
I have been wanting Dean more and more lately and
the more I think of him the more I want him.

My office is small and cozy and it's just the way I like
it. I didn't want anything flashy and over the top. I
just need a spot to work on reports and make sure
everyone is doing what they are supposed to do. I
started from where the calls come into first and made
my way through there first. The ones working in
dispatch are not getting the training they need and
there are notes in the files about time off.

I kept working through the mounds of paper and
seeing the same thing over and over again. Time off
and pay raises are not consistent. I check the clock
and notice it's 11:30 and realize I have plenty of time
to talk to Dave and see what was going on before a
jealous Dean came in, ready to go to lunch.

"Dave, can you come to my office?"

Dave walks in wearing dress slacks and a button up
and down white shirt. He is nothing to look at but he
is a nice man and very handsome. But he is no Dean.
Dean has the body of a god, and Dave, well, Dave has
a body.

"What's up babe?" Dave says as he enters the room.
I give him a weird look and then let it roll off like
water on a duck's back. I guess it's something he says

all the time and even though I don't like it, I'll address it later if it continues.

"I have a question about the vacation request and pay raises. It looks a little inconsistent." I show him what I'm talking about in the paperwork. The male employees are working the same amount of time and hours but are making less pay then the female employees. Also, their vacation requests are being denied more times than their female counterparts. I show Dave what I'm talking about and he walks over and leans in close to my body to look at the paper. He is a little too close for me.

"Well, I didn't know anyone kept records on that stuff." He says matter of fact.

What? You're the director, records are to be kept on everything.

"So why are you approving things for the female employees and not the male employees?" Dave leans back and props himself on the desk.

"You see." He grabs my hand and slowly caresses it as he continues speaking. "I make deals with the employees. They all know that they work under me. They also know, if they want to get ahead, they must go through me." He smiles as he squeezes my hand harder. "So, favors are granted by how hard the employee wants it." His grin grows sinister as he tries to pull my hand toward him.

"You creep!" I yell as I jerk my hand away. "You're a sick bastard!"

"Oh, don't say such mean things. I saw the way you looked at me the first day you came here. You smiled at me as you introduced everyone you were with. I knew you wanted me. I knew that you would call me in here before too long and want me to help you, *get ahead*."

"Get a head?" I step back from him as he starts stalking toward me. "I own this fucking company. Why do I need you?"

"You need me. You want me. I can see how you want to pull that little polka dotted skirt up and throw your blouse to the floor as you take my cock into that young. Pink. Pussy." Dave's almost on top of me, licking his lips. I try to move from one side, then the other, away from him but he grabs my arms and pins me to the ground. I fight as hard as I can against him but his strength is too much for me. He is as tall as Dean but he doesn't have the muscle tone like Dean at all and I think I can break free from him. He's still a lot bigger than I am though and I look at the clock on the wall and notice it's twelve o'clock. Dean should be coming through the door at any moment.

"Help me, someone help me. Dean, please help me."

I scream out. My door is shut and I'm sure everyone's at lunch.

"No one can hear you. Not even Dean, your so-called boyfriend." Dave's tongue slims across my cheek to my neck.

"You sick, bastard! Get off me!" I yell as he starts pushing my skirt up.

"I hope you're wct and ready for me, you little bitch." He tries to pull my panties off but I'm able to kick him in the stomach. I was aiming for a different spot, but missed. "You fucking bitch." Dave's hand slams across my face and the room starts spinning. He's going to rape me and there isn't a damn thing I, or anyone else can do about it. He is too strong and he has me pinned down.

"Oh, you're so fucking wet." Dave's fingers are back up my skirt pulling at my panties. My face is swelling from Dave's slap and I'm still seeing stars, but I'm able to feel him let go of my arm for a second while he tries to pull his slacks off.

"Get. OFF!" I scream as I hit Dave as hard as I can in the face with my free hand. It did little damage to his overpowering body.

"Feisty, I like that." The sick bastard is enjoying it when I fight him. His grin keeps growing more and more as he slaps me again. He pulls my hands above my head and holds them both there with one hand. "Yeah, fight me. Fight me you little bitch."

"Dean, Dean! Help me!" I keep calling out, hoping and praying that he will come to my rescue.

"Your boyfriend isn't coming. I made sure he was on a run. So, go ahead, scream all you want." Dave's sinister grin grows wider as he pushes his slimy body against mine. He made sure no one would hear me and that we were alone. I don't know how long he has been planning this out in his twisted mind. "Scream bitch. Scream!" Dave pulls his dick out of his pants and starts to spread my hips as wide as he can with his one free arm. He gives up trying to get my panties off and is hoping he can just push them aside. "Scream. Scre-." Mid-sentence Dave's body goes flying off me like he's pasta being thrown by an Italian chef.

Dean

I don't know what is going on and I really, don't give a fuck at this point. If Angelica is having sex with the director, then I'm going to kill him. If the director is trying to rape Angelica, well, I'm going to fucking kill him. Either way, Dave is about to get the shit knocked out of him and possibly die.

"Hold on Dean." The little weasel I just threw across the room starts saying with his hands held up in a pleading motion. "Hold on one-." He's trying to stand up with his dick hanging out and his pants down to his ankles. I turn my head sideways as I look at him, trying to figure out what explanation he can come up with. But whatever he is wanting to say, I'm not in the mood hear and I'm definitely not going to hold on. I catch the bastard across the jaw with my fist and his lip busts wide open. Blood spews all over his white shirt. "Son of bitch! Damn, Dean. Hold on. It's not what it looks like. She came onto me." Dave pulls at his pants trying to get them up over his bare ass as I stalk him down. I walk him backwards toward the door.

"You fucking liar!" Angelica is up off the ground holding her cheek were, I take it Dave's fist was before I walked in. "You tried to fucking rape me!" Her tone in her voice tells me all I need to know. She hates using the F word much and she always complains when I use it so freely. So, since she just dropped it a few times right now tells me she is not happy, I've been on the receiving end of those words before and it's not pretty. My blood boils as I feel my muscles tensing up in my body. Ok. *I'm going to fucking kill him.* I say to myself.

"That's not true. That slut tried to seduce me." Before he can finish his next set of lies I use his head to open the door the rest of the way and throw him on his ass into the hallway. Blood is still pouring from his lip as I hit him again in the jaw as he tries to stand. I can feel his jaw bone shatter as my fist makes contact. "Fuck. Listen to me. She tried to sleep her way to the top. Don't you care that your girlfriend is a whore?" I don't know if he thinks he is convincing me that Angelica was cheating on me, but either way, I'm still going to beat the shit out of him just because I want to now. I don't know where his logic is right now, why the hell would she need Dave to get to the top? Bethany and her own the fucking company.

"She's not my girlfriend. She's my fiancé." Dave's eyes widen as my fist make contact with his chin, sending him backwards through the bay doors. Everyone in the bay comes running out when they hear the commotion.

"Dean, calm down. Calm down one damn second." Dave is pleading for me to stop before I kill him and he knows he better either convince me fast or start running. "Think about your future here. I am your boss." Boss, who the fuck does he think he is, Angelica owns the fucking company. Does he not understand that? Maybe I hit him too hard and he can't comprehend what's going on. I look at Angelica to see if she is going to tell me to stop but she stands there with her hands on her hips.

"I own the FUCKING company, dickhead. I am **your** boss, the one you just tried to rape." Everyone in the bay looks on in awe as I continue my relentless assault on Dave.

"Your daddy owns this company. Not you. You don't own shit, you little rich princesses. **YOU DON'T OWN SHIT.** Your dad said I could run this company the way I want. Any, fucking way I want. He never had a problem with what I did with employees." Dave's eyes are red with anger as he threatens Angelica. I gather Dave isn't a smart man and he has gotten away with what he has been doing for years. Today will be the last day he will be doing what he wants too. He was trying to rape my fiancé and now he is insulting her by calling her names. Yeah. *I'm going to fucking kill him.*

"My dad is dead, you asshole. So yes. I do own SHIT. But not anymore, you're fired." Before Dave has time to let that fully set in, I pounce on him like a jungle cat. My fist never miss as Dave's head is turned into a punching bag. Blood is flying from my fist each time I pull them back for another ruthless blow. I don't plan on stopping until his face is caved in. I don't care if I kill the bastard or not. I am going to make sure he feels pain like he has never felt before. I am focused on Dave's head and that's it.

"Police. Stop." I hear a deep voice pronounce behind

me. I don't give a shit though as I hit Dave's face a few more times. They are going to have to pull me off my prey because I don't plan on stopping. When Dave stops breathing or stops moving then I will stop.

I feel an arm wrap around my waist and another around my legs. My fist is still contacting with Dave's face, even though two officers are pulling me off him.

"Calm down son. Calm down. It's over." The officers are pulling and holding me down with all their weight. Someone had called them and told them I just caught the little bastard trying to rape Angelica so, they know I'm not thinking right and they are there to help me more than Dave. I think of knocking them off me and going back on the attack, but think better of it when I see Dave's lifeless body lying on the ground. Dave won't be hurting anyone else anytime soon.

"We need a medic over here. NOW!" Another officer says as he kneels down to Dave's bloody body. "Dammit, we need a medic!" No one moves as the officer yells it louder this time. No one says anything even though the bay is full of medics and EMTs.

"I'm sorry officer, but the scene is not safe. We can't help Dave until the scene is safe." An older man with gold bars on his shirt says from the other side of the bay. "It's a protocol that Dave set up. I'm sorry."

Everyone in the bay looks as Dave lays motionless on the ground. No one seems to care if he is still breathing or if I beat the life out of the sorry bastard.

"Dean will not hurt anyone and Dave is no longer the Director. So, will someone please make sure my future husband and soon to be dad isn't a murder." Angelica's voice rings out, echoing through the bay.

"Did she just say, soon to be *dad?*" My head is spinning as I try to process what she just said. The officers are holding me down and I fill the pit of my stomach starting to turn. I think I'm going to puke. "*I'm going to be a dad?*" I repeat. The old man that spoke up just a minute ago jogs over to Dave's side and assesses the damage my fist did to his face.

"Some Bitch is still alive. Fuck!" The old man waves for more help and a couple of the others in the bay help to load Dave's tethered body in the back of an ambulance.

Angelica

"Soon to be dad?" Dean repeats as the officers still have him on the ground. His eyes grow wide as he processes the words and they start to sink in for him. I didn't mean to tell him like this but it just came out of my mouth. I took a pregnancy test a few days ago and when I saw the two-pink line I just about fainted. I've been wanting to tell him but I can't get my emotions in check to find the best time to talk to him about it. After I was in the hospital, I stopped taking my birth control but I didn't think anything about it until I started getting sick.

"I was going to tell you the other night before you left. I'm sorry I didn't tell you sooner." Tears are running down my cheek as Dean's face turns white. I was so scared the night Dean left that he would never come back at all and I didn't know what I would do without him. When he did come back, I forgot to tell him that I was pregnant. I wanted to tell him right away but he proposed to me and then everything was perfect and I was scared he would leave again.

"Ma'am, are you ok?" One of the officers asks as he tries to get my attention. I see him stepping between Dean and I but I'm only focused on Dean's face. "Ma'am?" He repeats louder.

"I'm fine. Dean saved me before Dave could do

anything. I am a little sore, but that's it." Everyone
in the bay is still looking on; afraid to move in case
there is more drama to come. My face is red from
Dave's hand where he slapped me and my wrist is
bruising from his tight grip.

"Angelica, oh my God. I'm so happy for you. Are
you sure you're ok, though?" Bethany comes running
up to me, throwing her arms around my neck and
nearly knocking me down. She has tears streaming
down her face like me.

"Well someone please take her to the hospital to be
checked out. NOW!" Dean is now pinned down by
three officers and he isn't liking it very much. No one
is moving after seeing what Dean just did to Dave and
Dean is starting to get mad again.

"I'm fine. I don't need to go." I argue with Dean but
her starts to push the officers off him to get to me and
I agree to go just so he won't do anything stupid.
He's already in a lot of trouble as it is and I don't
want him beating up officers so he can take me to the
hospital. "Fine. Bethany, will you take me?" Adam
and Aaron walk up and hold on to my arm to lead me
to their Ambulance.

"We will take you. If that's OK with you and Dean?
Our ambulance is right there. You can ride with us
too if you want Bethany." Dean's face shows his
approval of the brothers taking care of me. Of course,

I don't think anyone would try anything after watching Dean nearly kill Dave.

The brothers help me into the ambulance and as we drive away I see Dean finally being stood up and placed in handcuffs.

I was at the hospital for less than an hour before they told me I could go home. Everything looked fine and the baby wasn't hurt during the assault. I have a big knot in my stomach for not telling Dean that I was pregnant sooner, but after everything we have been through, I thought it would be best to not tell him just yet. Seeing him nearly kill Dave for trying to rape me, makes me know that Dean loves me with all his heart and that he will try to protect me and the baby, no matter what.

Bethany and I were picked up by Adam and Aaron again and they drove us home. Dean isn't there to greet us at the front door and the house seems so bare without him. We both walk in and fall on the couch, ready for the day to be over. I know it is far from being over though once Dean does get home, if he is released tonight.

The front door springs open and Dean walks in with a big grin on his face.

"Dean, oh my God. You're home. I've missed you. What happened? What did the police say?" He never misses a step as he crosses the room toward me. His rock-hard arms wrap around my waist as he lifts me in the air as he presses his lips to mine and holds me tight against his body.

"I love you. I'm so sorry I was late for lunch." How could he be sorry for that? He saved me, again. He is always saving me.

"It's not your fault Dean. Now tell me, what did the police say." His eyes are full of tears as he lets my feet touch the ground again. He kneels to one knee and places a kiss on my stomach. I can't hold back my feelings for him any longer. I want him. I want him right here and now. I have seen Dean be sweet before and nice, but he has a different look to him right now.

"Take me, Dean." I whisper in his ear but he doesn't move a muscle. "Fuck me. Now!" I have used that word too many times today but I want Dean to know that I'm not playing. I need him inside me, right now. His face lights up as the words roll off my tongue and hits his ear drum. I can see the shockwave of emotion shoot through his body as he thinks of taking me on the couch.

"But you're pregnant. I can't do that to you." I smile as he thinks of me being pregnant with his child.

"The doctor said I'm fine. Now take me before I

explode." Dean wraps his arms around me and cradles me in his arms. My feet never touch the ground as we head toward the bedroom. I was going to tell Bethany she needed to find another room to relax in but Dean has other plans for me. I wave at Bethany as he carries me off for a night of passion. She smiles and mouths to me to have fun. Dean lays my back against the soft king size bed and kisses my neck. His hand slides up my inner thigh to my wetness. He can feel how excited I am through my panties and I want him to enjoy me all night long.

Dean

The police were not happy with me beating Dave half to death, but they were very understanding that I was protecting Angelica. They were not going to file any charges on me since so many women came forward and accused him of rape or exchanging sex for favors. I was glad that Angelica waited to tell me she was pregnant while the cops had me on the ground and not while I was pounding Dave's face in. I think I would have snapped Dave's neck if I knew it beforehand.

"Good morning baby." I wrap my arms around Angelica's waist and feel her belly. "And good morning little guy."

"How do you know it's a boy? We might be having a little girl." Angelica smiles and places her hands-on mine.

"Fine then. Good morning Prince or Princess." I say as I tighten my grip on her even more. I don't care if it's a boy or a girl, as long as they are healthy, I'm good with either.

"That's better. Thank you." She lays her head over on my chest and I don't want the morning to end. "I'm hungry." She says just as I'm getting comfortable snuggling against her.

I spring from the bed running toward the kitchen

yelling, "What do you want?" She thought I was over protective before, just wait.

"So, what happened with the police, are you in any trouble?" We didn't talk very much last night. After I got home, we had sex so many times we both passed out from exhaustion.

"Everything is fine. I was told that Dave has been a person of interest for a while in few assaults and rapes. They said to stay out of trouble and we wouldn't hear any more about it." I knew there was something strange about Dave when we first met him, but I wasn't sure what it was. I didn't want to bring it up though and there was no way I would say, *told you so*. Even though I really wanted to, but I don't want to be a dick about it. Dave was a sick bastard and if I'd been at her office when I said I was going to be, then her face wouldn't be black and blue this morning.

We ate breakfast and Angelica started to feel sick after a few bites. I guess morning sickness is no joke. We walk down to the beach to enjoy the tide rolling in and the sunrise. I don't know how I lived so many years and never took time to sit and enjoy the sound of the water. I feel at peace with the world and with my life. Angelica thought it would be best if we took a few days off from work and I was good with that. I really didn't care if we ever went back to work but she wants to for some reason. She wasn't sure how everyone would treat me, after I beat the hell out of their last boss and I have their new one pregnant with my baby.

"Do you want to have a party here? Instead of having a bachelor or bachelorette party? We can invite some of the ones from EMS and just have a fun time sitting on the beach." Angelica has a great idea and it can be a way to keep both of us safe. I don't know how long she has been thinking about having a party or where the thought came from. I guess that's how her pregnant brain works though. I don't like the idea of her going out to party with her friends and watch them get drunk while she has to watch.

"That sounds great. But when do you want to get married?" My heart stops as I wait for her to answer me.

A lifetime passes since I asked her when she wanted to get married.

It seems like a lifetime passes as she thinks about my question. I stare into her eyes, hoping she still wants to marry this overprotective guy in front of her. I know I want to marry her before the baby is born but I want her to make the decision. I'm ok waiting also if she wants too.

"How about before the baby?" She smiles as she asks to see if I approve. "Let's say six months? We will know the sex of the baby and all worrying will be over. Then we can relax and have a small ceremony here on the beach." I kiss her head and hold her tight to my chest.

"That sounds perfect." I say as I squeeze her tight.

Now that the wedding date has been set and our party is going to happen next month I feel like I can breathe easier. Everything is going great and is on track for once in our life. Since the incident with Dave happened two months ago, Angelica and I have been working at EMS a lot. She's taken over the director position with Bethany and they are up to their necks in back paperwork. I try to help them some, but I'm needed on the truck more than anything. Runs are coming in left and right and we never have a free day together anymore.

"Dean, where are you?" Angelica asks. It's about time for me to be off from work but I was just sent on a run. That's been my luck for the past few weeks. Her and Bethany have had to leave me at work and go on home because of late runs.

"I'm heading out to a possible shooting outside of town. I think it's close to where the old research lab was." I don't remember a lot of where things were ten years ago and I really don't care if I ever do. The town was once big when the lab was open, but since they closed it, everyone has moved away.

"Just be careful. Come home safe to me. Promise me." I can hear how worried she is in her voice and I know she thinks something bad is going to happen to me. But after all that we've both been through, I'm ready for anything.

"I will honey. I love you. I have to go. We're pulling up."

I hang up as we pull in where the shooting took place. Police cars litter the streets and no one seems happy to be here.

"What do we have?" I yell at one of the police officers as I get out of the ambulance with my partner. The old man that helped Dave was riding with me today and he hasn't said much to me all shift.

"Don't right know yet." The officer responds looking down at the bodies. "Looks like a robbery gone wrong. But it's hard to tell." There's a man and woman lying on the ground shot to death. Their wallets and IDs were stolen and there's no trace of anything else taken from the victims.

"That's odd." I lift the man's arm up to show the officer his watch. "That's a ten-thousand-dollar watch. This isn't a robbery gone wrong unless it was the dumbest robber in history." Something's odd with the fact that both victim's personal jewelry wasn't removed. Only wallets. Someone was after more than just money. Someone picked these people for a reason.

"Mr. and Mrs. However you say that last name." The officer spells a long German last name for me. I remember the name, I thought they were scientists that worked with my parents but I can't be sure.

My heart sinks in my chest. Could Gloria and Gabriela know we are here? Could they be looking for us again? My mind goes a million different ways as I try to think of what I'm going to tell Angelica. Nothing. I'm not going to tell her anything. Maybe these two people were killed for some other reason and there is no reason to scare her. She doesn't need that much stress right now.

"Dean," one of the officers that was holding me down when I attacked Dave, called out for me. "Dean, let me talk to you."

"What's up?" I say, not knowing what he had on his mind.

"That prick that you about killed, he's gone." My chest tightens and I know there must be a connection now.

"What do you mean gone?" I tried to sound like I'm not worried, but right now I'm scared to death.

"When he got out of the hospital, he disappeared. We don't know what happened to him. I don't know if he got scared and ran or what." I didn't know Dave at all, but after seeing him try to rape my fiancée, I doubt he ran scared.

"Well, if I see him or hear of where he might be, I'll call you first. I understand what you did and none of us here blame you for doing it. We're sorry for being rough with you that day." The officer smiles and shakes my hand. I'm still processing the fact that Dave is on the loose. "Dean, just don't do anything stupid if he seeks you all out. I think you might kill him this time if you get a hold of him." You damn right I will. If Dave shows his ass, I will kill him where he stands.

Angelica

Dean told me about the German couple that had been killed by the lab. He didn't want to tell me at first, but I made him tell me what the run was about. I heard the page out right before Bethany and I headed home. I broke down crying on the phone and he swore he would protect me. I know he will try but I hate the thought of someone trying to kill us all over again.

"Dean, just be careful. What if Gloria and Gabriela found us and are planning on trying to kill us both again?" He knows I'm upset and I didn't want him to worry about me all the time, but it worries me that one of them might try to drug Dean and use him again. Now that we are about to start a family, I worry about everything.

"I promise I will watch out. I love you, Angelica and nothing can take me from you. Please don't worry about me. Just stay safe and call me or the police if anything seems odd."

He's right. I don't need to worry about things that I can't control.

Weeks fly by and everything's quiet and we haven't heard any more about the shooting. Maybe it was nothing and we were worrying for no reason, but it still had us all on edge. The police said that Dave disappeared and they're not sure where he might be hiding out either. They have warrants out for his arrest and told us to call them if we hear where he is.

Everything is slowly starting to get back to normal and Bethany is looking forward to the beach party. We planned on inviting everyone from EMS and some of the police officers that we know as well.

Dean thought it might be a good way to say thank you to a few of them. They have been watching our crews closely and we have even had an officer stay at base to make sure Dave doesn't come back.

"Dean, are you ready for tonight?" I ask him, knowing the answer to the question before it ever leaves my lips. He wants to take me to the bedroom and hide out for a few months and take advantage of my preger hormones. I'm horny, all the time and he loves it. Dean stopped by my office last week to tell me something and we ended up on top of my desk like he wanted my first day of work. I can't stop myself though.

"Not really. Do we really have to hang out with everyone?" I know Dean is joking, sort of. He wants to have a nice get together to prove that nothing is going to happen and that we are all safe. But if it is one thing I have learned about Dean Mason, it is that he worries. His eyes give him away when he is deep in thought about something and tonight they are distant with worry.

"It won't be long. We might be able to slip away and have some fun." I run my hands down to his crotch. "If you're a good boy." Dean shoots to attention and yells.

"I'll be good!" I know he would anyways, but I love to feel him get hard and then walk away. It's fun teasing him.

The party is going well and Bethany is finding that the brothers, Adam and Aaron, are fun to be around. I think it's more of the fact that she is tipsy and they are good looking. She's been giving them signals that a blind person could see but I don't think they have noticed yet. Dean and I slipped off toward the house after a couple hours and I let him have fun with my cravings. We tell everyone to stay as long as they want to.

Dean

"Thank you." Angelica lays her head on my chest.

"For?" I'm just waking up and a little confused on why she is thanking me so early in the morning.

"Last night was fun. It was nice to have friends here for a party. Thank you for agreeing to it."

"No problem. Do you know who all's still here or have you been out yet?" I figure Bethany still had the brothers in her room. Even though her room was on the other side of the house, we still heard them all night long. I understand how Bethany feels when she hears us all the time. I thought a few others might be hanging around and sleeping last night off but I wasn't sure.

"I got up earlier to check. Bethany still has the brothers with her, but everyone else has left." Angelica leans up and kisses my lips. "And you're still here."

I smile and kiss her back. "I'm not going anywhere. Except to clean. I bet this place is a mess." I walk out of the bedroom and noticed that I was right. Beer bottles litter everywhere there is a flat surface. There are clothes lying outside and some panties hanging from a lamp shades. I don't want to know what all went on last night and I don't care.

"Good morning guys." I say to Adam and Aaron as they walk out of Bethany's room looking for the rest of their clothes. Both are wearing shorts and no shirt and I can see Bethany's fingernail marks all across their backs and chest. I knew from the screaming last night, they were having a wild time but seeing them confirms it.

"Um, good morning sir." Both look like hell and they keep their heads down as embarrassment is starting to set in.

"Sounded like you two had a fun night." I say, laughing, as I walk outside to start cleaning up the mess on the beach.

The brothers didn't stick around much longer after they found their shirts. Bethany tried her hardest to get them back in the bedroom for some more fun, but Angelica reminded them that they have a shift today. My next shift isn't for a few more days and I'm happy about that.

Angelica has a doctor's appointment to see what the sex of the baby is and I'm not missing it for nothing. I spent the morning cleaning what was left over from the party and filled up five garbage bags with trash.

After the house is halfway put back together, we head out to Pensacola. I can't wait to know what we are having. Angelica asked me the other day if I wanted a boy or a girl. I don't care either way. The only thing that I care about is whether or not the baby is healthy.

Angelica is wearing a blue sundress and she looks beautiful in it. She said it's easier with her ever-growing belly and boobs to fit into too. I'm not complaining about the dress or the growing belly and boobs. I think she looks more beautiful each day. I love how much sex we have been having lately as well. I wish she would stay pregnant all the time, the sex is amazing and she is horny all the time.

"Ms. Muller, we're ready for you." The nurse says as she motions for us to follow her. My heart's racing and I think I'm going to be sick. The nurse has her change clothes and lay down on a table, exposing her baby bump.

"The ultrasound tech and doctor will be right in."

"Are you nervous?" Angelica says as she takes my hand.

"Yes. Yes, I am." We both laugh at my honesty, but I'm more scared than anything. What if something's wrong? What if the cord is around the baby's neck, what if the heart isn't beating right? What if?

"Dean. Breathe. It'll be ok." Angelica squeezes my hand tight. I guess I had the "OH SHIT" look on my face and she knew what I was running through my mind.

Two young women come in and set up a machine with a magical wand to see the baby. They turn the lights off and apply a ton of gel to her stomach. Neither women say much as they scan around looking at the baby. They take measurements and print off pictures as they go, but other than that, they don't say anything. They turn on Doppler so we can hear the baby's heartbeat.

"That is the best sound in the world." We say to each other. I'm amazed at how much the little one looks like a baby and not an alien anymore.

"Look right there. You see that?" The tech says, while pointing at the screen.

"No, No I don't." I say as I strain my eyes to see what the hell she's talking about.

"Right there." She points again to something bright on the screen. "There are three bright lines there. You know what that means?"

"I hope to God not triplets." Angelica slaps my arms as she turns and examines the picture for herself.

"Does that mean? We're going to have a girl?" My heart stops. A girl. I'm so fucked.

"Yes it does sweetie."

"Oh my God." Angelica starts tearing up and I can't hold it back either.

"Oh, shit!" I say and Angelica gives me a dirty look. "I. I love you honey. I love you so much. But, shit!" Nothing else will come out. I can't believe we're having a little girl. My life is going to be turned upside down if she is anything like me.

The doctor tells us that everything looks great and that within two months Angelica should be delivering. We can't decide on a name yet, but we know it will come to us soon enough.

"I can't wait." I tell her as we're driving home. Angelica is staring at the pictures of the little princess that she's growing inside her. Once we get home I hold her tight. We're relaxing on the back porch, watching the waves and listening to them crash around us. Nothing can be better.

"I need to tell you something." Angelica says.

Anything she wants to tell me can't ruin the mood I'm in. I shake my head and wait for her to talk.

"Do you remember anything from when you were here with your parents?" I haven't tried to remember anything but no. They died so suddenly, that I don't want to think of it anymore. I smile and shake my head no.

"I think of my mom all the time. She worked with your parents a lot and she knew you. She always told me that you were special. I never knew what she was talking about, until I saw you going into work to get your job back. I always knew you hung around me but you never tried to talk to me. You were older and I figured you didn't want anything to do with me anyway. But she always saw something that I couldn't. She always said that, you would be the one to help me one day. That you would be the one to save me. I thought my dad would be the one to help me, but he was too weak." She lays her head over on my chest and sucks in a deep breath and then lets it out slowly. Her warm exhale tickles my chest hair. "I guess what I'm trying to say is that I have loved you, longer than I've known it."

I don't know how to answer her on that one so I just squeeze her tighter to my chest for a minute. I do remember her and her mom and I remember my parents telling me about how her dad left them. I always wanted to talk to the little blonde that looked so cute and innocent, but I was afraid of what she would think of me. My parents died the same day I built up the courage to speak to her and after that, I stopped thinking about this place or anyone associated with it. I moved away and was found by Roxanna and she taught me a new way to suppress my pain. I would use one night stands to dull the pain of being alone. I vowed to never give myself to anyone. I couldn't. I thought that Roxanna was the one a long time ago that I would be with her but she was just a means to forget the pain as well. My heart belonged to my parents and when they died, so did it.

When I met Angelica though, I found an Angel. I didn't remember her at first but when I found out who she was, it made sense why I'm drawn to her. She's the one that I've always loved.

"I have never felt like this toward anyone since my parents died. All of the sex, drinking, and everything else is nothing compared to the comfort I get from having you near me. I thought I found love in Gabriela and thought that she was the one. But when I met you, I knew right away that you were the one. I remember watching the little cute blonde girl playing with her mom while I sat, bored with my parents. I always wanted to talk to you and play with you. I never knew I was watching my future wife and mother of my kid play." I hold on to her tight as she snuggles to my chest as my eyes start watering. I think of how proud my parents would be right now.

Bethany

"911, where's your emergency?"

"Help me, Please, God. Help."

"Where are you Ma'am?"

"I'm at Sapphire Coast at the Beach house of Angelica Muller's." I say, trying to hide in the darkness.

"Who are you calling you whore, give me that fucking phone."

"No, no!" I scream and scream as I fight to get help on the line. "Stop! Stop!"

"Bang!"

"Ma'am, are you there? Was that a gunshot? Ma'am?" The 911 operator is screaming on the phone.

"I told you what would happen. Did you really think Dean could insult me like that and I wouldn't come back for him?" The deep voice echoes through my head.

"Help me, please help me!" I scream again through the phone, praying that someone can hear me.

"Bang! Bang!" More gun shots ring out somewhere

242

in the house.

"All units be advised; I am hearing multiple gun shots. I repeat. Shots fired at the location." 911 is still trying to get my attention, as I lay on the ground with blood coming from my head and mouth. I refuse to let go of the phone though. Blood is soaking the floor in the living room and more is on the walls around me.

"Please don't let me dic. I don't want to die. Please." I cry into the phone, not knowing if anyone's still listening.

"No, stay away. No." Angelica's voice becomes distant as the attacker is on top of her.

"We started a game and I never got to finish. There's no one to stop me this time." Angelica tries to fight but she's being overpowered by the large frame on top of her. I try moving to help her as I push my fist to the floor and push with all my strength to stand up. My legs feel weak from the blood I've lost and I'm not sure how much longer I have before I pass out. "GET OFF MY SISTER!" I scream, throwing what little weight I have at him.

8 hours earlier

Dean

The wedding is going to be in a few days and I am ready. I can't wait for angelica to be Mrs. Mason. I'm tired of hearing her called Ms. Muller all the time. Bethany's going to be her maid of honor and I've been trying to think of someone to be my best man. I thought of calling Detective Moore and seeing if he would come up for the wedding but I'm not sure if Angelica would like it. He's known her for years and seems like a good guy. I asked Angelica if she wants someone to give her away, since her dad isn't alive anymore, but she said she is independent and could walk by herself. She's strong willed like that and stubborn.

I pull out my cell phone and go through my contacts until I find him. "Detective Moore."

"Dean. What's going on? Long time since I've heard from you. How's everything going?" He sounds cheaper for it being early in the morning.

"Angelica and I are getting married in a few days and I wanted to know if you would like to be my best man?" There's a long pause from him.

"I'd love to man. I'm just now getting off work and

will be off for the weekend. Do you care if I go ahead and come on up?"

"I'd love that. We are at Angelica's mom's beach house. Do you know where that is?"

"Yep, be there in like eight hours."

After hanging up I debate whether telling Angelica about Detective Moore coming to the wedding or just leaving it for a surprise. We all took off from work for a few days so we could prepare for the big day. We aren't going to do anything big for the wedding, but the weather is going to be nice, so we decided to have it on the beach. We are going to use the house for the reception.

Purple is the theme and it's everywhere. Everything's being delivered around the clock and I can't believe that I'm going to be married. The past year has flown by so fast and I feel like we're rushing into marriage, but it feels right. Angelica's pregnant and we're about to start a family of our own. I want to be the father and husband that I remember my dad being. I know Angelica wishes her dad would have stuck around after her mom got sick, but she told me that the first nine years of her life were perfect. Her dad took her places and played with her. I tell her about my parents taking me to Disney World and she says she would love to go there sometime. We were both shocked to find out that Bethany was her sister. It's good for them though because they both have each other and there's nothing that's going to tear them apart. I think they both needed a sister.

"Dean, Bethany and I are going out for a day of pampering, are you sure you'll be ok by yourself?" Angelica asks as she stands with Bethany in the doorway. Both are in shorts and tanks for their spa day. I never realized before how much they look the same, the only difference now is Angelica's belly. Every now and again it looks like a wave pool. The little girl inside kicking and twisting, and I see Angelica smile as she places her hand on her stomach to feel her. I can't wait to hold our precious little Angel.

"I'll be fine. Take your time. I love you." I give her a big kiss and kiss her belly before walking her out to Bethany's car. "What time will you be back?"

"Later this afternoon. Don't worry about us. We have a full day of spa and relaxation planned. I love you." Her words would calm a raging storm and I feel relieved that Bethany is going to be with her today. I don't have a lot of stuff to do except wait on delivery guys, so I'm going to relax on the beach.

I watch as the two, or I should say three, girls pull out of the drive and leave me home alone. I'm ready for a relaxing day of sun and beach.

Angelica

Bethany and I are going to treat ourselves to a day at the spa, and we are ready. My feet are swelling and I feel measurable. Even though I look as big as a whale, Dean's eyes still light up when I walk in the room. I can't wait to be Mrs. Mason. I'm young and sheltered from a lot of stuff but I know Dean loves me with all his heart and that he will protect me at all cost.

I slip out of bed and go to find Dean. He must have woken before me and is getting everything ready for our big day. I don't know if he's as nervous as I am but I hope not.

"Detective Moore." I hear Dean's sexy voice say in the other room. I stop in my tracks and wait to hear what he is calling him for. Did he find out more about that couple that was murdered? What is he doing?

"Angelica and I are getting married in a few days and want to know if you would be my best man?" My heart stops as the question leaves Dean's lips.

"Say no, say no, say no." I whisper as I listen. I can't believe he's asking him to be his best man. I called him the other day and told him that we were getting married. He was less than thrilled but said he would be there if I wanted him too. I told him that if Dean says something about it then I would be ok with it. But, what if Dean finds out about him? What will he do? Will he still marry me?

"I'd love that. We are at Angelica's mom's beach house. Do you know where that is?" Oh, my God. My heart sinks as I know he agreed to come up for the wedding. I really hoped Dean would not invite him but I can't stop him now. This is going to screw everything up.

Dean hangs up the phone and walks outside to sign for more catering things that keep pouring in.

"Oh God. I'm fucked now." I say out loud.

"Why are you fucked?" Bethany is standing behind me and I gasp when I turn around. "Angelica, are you having second thoughts?" She says smiling at me.

"No. I. I just." Should I tell her? Should I confide in her about Detective Moore coming? She knows the story. Sort of. I never told her that he was a Detective. "I-."

"Sis, I understand. You're nervous. Just calm down." She wraps her arms around my neck and hugs me tight. It feels nice to have a sister. Someone that understands me and that I can talk to, or not talk to. "Have you heard yet who Dean is getting for his best man?" I freeze, every muscle in my body stiffens and I can't believe she's asking. Did she hear him, too?

"Yeah, sort of." I say. My heart is racing at the thought of Detective Moore coming to the house.

"Who, who? Tell me. Who is it? Is he cute? Is he single?" Bethany's holding me by the shoulders and almost shaking me to get me to talk.

"Dean doesn't know that I know. But. It's Detective Moore." I say shakily.

Bethany laughs. "So, I thought you were friends?"

"Detective Moore is my friend. But he is also Richard." I feel as though I can throw up now and it's not morning sickness this time.

Bethany's eyes widen and the corners of her mouth turn up. "He doesn't know?"

"No. I never told Dean how and why I knew him."

"You never told me he was a Detective. You little-." Bethany hugs me and grins even more. "Well. This will be fun."

"Shut up." I say as I push her away. "Let's get dressed. And don't you dare say a word to Dean about him."

"Wouldn't dream of it sis." We both head to our

rooms to find something comfortable to wear for our spa day. Short and a tank sounds good to me. I'm ready for a long day of pampering.

"Dean, Bethany and I are going out for a day of pampering, are you sure you'll be ok by yourself?" I ask, standing with Bethany by the door. Dean's watching both of us and I can feel the little girl kicking me. I place my hand on my belly. *You know your daddy's watching you.* Oh, it feels nice.

"I'll be fine. Take your time. I love you." He gives me a big kiss and kisses my belly before walking us out to Bethany's car. "What time will you be back?"

"Later this afternoon. Don't worry about us. We have a full day of spa and relaxation planned. I love you." I try not to sound nervous and I don't want him to know I heard him on the phone earlier. I can't believe Detective Moore, I mean Richard, is coming. God, I'm so fucked.

We wave as Bethany pulls out on the drive. My phone starts buzzing and I grab it fast to open. Dean's probably wanting to tell me he loves me again and that he misses me.

"Are you missing me already?"

"Well, now that you say it, yes." A deep voice says over the phone.

"Richard. What the hell do you want?" Bethany turns and smiles at me.

"Is that anyway to greet me? And when did you start cursing so much?" Richard laughs on the phone as I want to reach through it and strangle him. "I just want to tell you, your fiancé asked me to be his best man. I'm headed your way now. Are you ok with this? Or, do I need to call and tell him work just called me in?" I can't do that to Dean, but I also can't have him finding out the truth either.

"Will you be on your best behavior?" I ask with a stern tone.

"Promise pumpkin."

"Don't call me that. You know that was a long time ago." I snap at him.

"Testy aren't we, must be the baby hormones. After everything I've done for you, this is how you treat me. Fine, I will be good. I take it he doesn't know then?"

"No. And let's keep it that way." I tell him, gripping the phone tighter.

"Fine. Have it your way. You know he'll understand. You were young and I-"

"Shut the fuck up before I change my mind."

"What a dirty mouth." He says as he laughs even harder. "See you soon, Angelica. I can't wait." I drop my phone back in my purse.

"Shit! Shit, fuck, damn, shit, son of a fucking bitch, fucking shit!" I yell.

"Something wrong?" Bethany says while smiling at me.

"You think it's funny?"

"Sort of. I assume that was Detective Moore?" Her mischievous grin is bigger than normal.

"What do you think?"

"You should have told him. He told you about me. You should have told him about." She turns and seductively says, "RICHARD."

I'm screwed. Completely. When Dean finds out who Richard really is and how we know each other. I'm screwed. He'll leave. "Should I call him and tell him who Richard is? Should I throw it out there now?" My hands are clasped around my face as I try to think of a solution.

"I wouldn't just yet. Don't worry about it. Your secret is safe with me. I won't tell him and he never has to know. I'm sure there are things in his past he doesn't want you to know about." She's right. I'm sure there are things he doesn't want to tell me about or people he'd rather me not meet one day.

Spa day is just what I need and I'm glad Bethany's going to spend the whole day with me. Dean's been driving me crazy at the house and I want to get away for a little while and not have to listen to him for once. He won't let me do anything around the house. He's so afraid that I'll get hurt.

"So where to first?" I ask Bethany, who has been driving like a mad woman across town.

"First is massages and then mani and pedi."

"Ow, that sounds good."

"Then we go for our hair and then drinks by the water and that's the day."

"You know I can't drink." I say slapping her arm.

"I know, I know. But I can." Her evil smile shines through and I laugh at her.

"If I can't drink. You can't drink."

"You suck sis."

We pull into a small parking lot that has the sign "Tropical Spa," written on a big billboard. It's a nice building with palm trees surrounding it and bright pinks and other colors dancing through everywhere. I giggle thinking of what it looks like inside, since it's so bright out here.

When we walk in through a single glass door, the feeling is the same. Slow Japanese music plays over the PA and a waterfall next to the cash register trickles down. Chairs where we'll be getting our nails done look like the fanciest leather ever made. I think I could sleep in one for the rest of my life, and be happy.

"Hello, welcome to Tropical Spa, where your oasis is our pleasure." A young Asian girl says, with a little accent.

"Hi, we're here for a spa treat-."

"Brooks, I called the other day and we have an appointment." Bethany interrupts me mid-sentence.

"Aw, yes. Bethany and Angelica. And Angelica, pregnant bride to be? YES?" The young girl asks. Her long black hair is pulled back in a ponytail, but it still stretches past her butt. She's short and skinny with shorts and a plain shirt on. Nothing fancy whatsoever.

"Ah. Yes." I say, not sure if she's asking a question or making a statement.

"This way, this way. Come, come." She takes us to a private room that has the same style of music playing, it sounds like someone picking at a small guitar. There are two large tables that face another waterfall that cascades down the side of the wall. I smile at the sound of the water and think of camping trips my mom and dad would take me on when I was little. The stream was always filled with rocks and at night I could hear the trickle. The lights are dim and the air smells of burning incense. I know this has to be heaven.

"Lay down for me here and pregnant lady, you lay on this one. It's special for your belly and won't hurt you. If you start to feel pain, just let us know."

"Thank you."

When I lay down and close my eyes, I remember the way my mom's long blonde hair would fall in her face when the wind blew. She was beautiful. I mainly look like her and sometimes it's hard to look in the mirror without tearing up.

"Isn't this great?" Bethany's lying face down, melting into the tables, waiting for the magical hands to be on her body. We stripped off our clothes and only had a small towel over our waist.

"I couldn't dream of anything better." I hear the door open and two male voices speaking to each other quietly. They're gathering their lotions and oils and are deciding who is going to massage who.

I feel the hot oil hit my bare back and I tense under the pleasure. Aw, it feels nice. My muscles began to cry out in pleasure from the hot oil as two strong hands push down on my back. Sliding and pushing the oil from my butt to my neck. The only thing covering me is the small towel and I feel vulnerable under the strong hands covering my body. I think of Dave and his hands holding me down. I want to move and get up but the hands aren't forcing me down, but instead, they are forcing the stress from my body. I never open my eyes to see who's doing this wonderful thing to my body and I don't care. Everything aches from the pregnancy and every joint is swelling as my due date quickly approaches.

"You ok over there, sis?" Bethany heard my cries of pleasure and is making sure that I'm still with her.

"Yes." I stutter.

"Let it out girl. That's what these guys are here for. Well, mine might get to do more than just my back and legs." My face turns red as I try not to think of Bethany riding a complete stranger, next to me.

The hands once again hit my upper thighs and I scream this time as I'm very sensitive to any touch.

"You ok?" The young girl comes running into the room asking.

"I'm sorry. The pregnancy has my hormones all out of whack." I bit my lip trying not to look too turned on as I hold the sheet across my chest looking at the young girl and the muscle man that's wearing tight white shorts and a white button and down shirt that's four sizes too small. I grin and bite the sheet as I feel heat rush across my face.

"It's ok. It happens a lot. AJ's used to it. Just let self-go and let him take care of everything." She turns and shuts the door again and I sink back down to the table. I feel AJ's hands go back on my body and my body begins its journey again to the top.

After a full hour of pleasure and me screaming for joy a half dozen times, it was time for the mani and pedi. I've never had one before and am nervous. Letting someone else control my hands while I sit and watch them work effortlessly on my hands and feet; it never sounded like fun to me.

The chairs that I now want for a new bed are as soft as they look. Once I'm laid back, feeling water rush around my feet, a woman starts working on my hands. Pushing back at the nails and cleaning everything. I wince in pain to begin with but am able to overcome the discomfort after a few minutes.

"Where have you been?" I ask Bethany as she walks into the main part of the building and flops in the chair next to me.

"Ah. My massage took a little longer." She pulls her shoulders up and grins at me. By the way her hair is all matted up and she's giggling, I have a pretty good guess what was being massaged.

"Yeah, well this is a spa day. Not fuck a stranger day."

"You are picking up some bad habits from me sis." She smiles at the fact that I have used the F word a ton already today and it's still early. "No more, I promise." She holds up her hands. I laugh and go back to watching the girl work on my hands. She would massage them and then cause the worst pain ever to them. Then she would go back to massaging them again. It's a vicious cycle. When she reaches my feet, it isn't any better. I cry out a few times as my swollen ankles are hurting from the constant attention they are getting.

Bethany paid the little woman at the front that checked us in and waved by to AJ and his look alike. I guess one wasn't enough to please her today.

We head across town to the hair salon and I'm ready for my scalp to be massaged as much as the rest of my body just was. Bethany has everything planned and there is no waiting to be seen when we walk in. Everyone jumps when we walk in and take us to where we need to go. When the girl lays my chair back and starts rinsing my hair, I forget about everything else. Nothing in the world matters to me right now. I am relaxing for once. Her nails are scrubbing my scalp as she rinses and shampoos my hair.

"Sweetheart? Sweetheart? Are you ok?" My eyes are not wanting to open and I can hear Bethany and the other women around trying to wake me up.

"There, now she's coming around. How do you feel Angelica?" Bethany's kneeling down beside me as a man in a gray uniform checks my blood pressure.

"What the hell happened? Who are you?" I push the man from my arm and try to fight with Bethany to let me up.

"Calm down, sis. You passed out. We called 911 and the ambulance is here checking you out. It's Adam and Aaron. They said your blood pressure dropped and your blood sugar is low. Also, something about the pressure of the baby was cutting blood flow off. That's why you passed out."

"Oh, my God. Is the baby-''

"Angelica, the baby is fine, just try to calm down. We were about to call Dean, but you started waking up. Do you still want us to call him for you?" Adam's taking his equipment off me and Aaron has his phone out ready to dial.

"No, no. If you say I'm ok, then I'm ok. I might just need to rest. I hate to worry him about nothing." Everyone stares at me like I'm crazy as I try to convince them that I'm fine now.

"Ok, if you need us, just call us. We'll gladly take you anywhere you need us too." I've noticed that since Bethany and I started working and owning the ambulance service, the guys have been a lot nicer to patients, but today, they were exceptional. It makes me feel proud to know that they are treating everyone with respect and not pushing anyone to go to the hospital. Of course, I also know, they don't want to screw up in front of their bosses.

"Angelica, you should call Dean. What if he finds out? He will be worried sick." Bethany has a point, but I don't want to bother him.

"We've been gone for almost six hours, let's just finish with our hair and then head back. I will tell him when I get there. Deal?"

Bethany nods, even though she isn't happy about it.

We finished our hair and I promised Bethany she could have one drink down by the water before we head back. The sunset is beautiful, with the amber glow coming across the sky. We sit on the water's edge and I drank water, while she has a Mojito. The smell of the ocean breeze makes any worry dissipate.

"That's odd." Bethany says, looking at her phone.

"What?" I say rolling my eyes at her.

"Your future husband didn't text me back. I told him about your little episode and he hasn't text back."

"Maybe he's busy." I say, trying not to sound too pissed at her for telling him. "And why the hell did you tell him anyway?"

"He has a right to know. But, the strange part is that it shows he read it thirty minutes ago. You would think he would have called or something."

"Well, call him." I say pointing to her phone. Bethany taps on her screen and holds the phone up to her ear. I can hear it ringing and ringing. Then I hear it pick up and then disconnect.

"Odd." Bethany tries again. This time she places the phone in the middle of the table and puts it on speaker. It rings and rings and rings. Then it picks up again and what sounds like a girl's voice says something, then the phone goes dead again. "That's odd."

"We probably need to get back. What if he's in trouble?" I remember the last time I called Dean's phone and a woman answered it. He was being tortured and electrocuted, before being left to burn alive.

"But." Bethany starts to finish her question and then shakes her head. I'm not sure what she is thinking but I am worried about him and want to make sure he is ok. "We can make it there in about ten minutes. Do you want me to call the police?"

"No. Let's go check on him. I'm sure it's nothing." I say. Hoping that I'm not just lying to myself. I start to stand up and I feel a sharp pain go through my stomach to my back. I let out a scream and Bethany grabs my arm.

"Are you ok? Do I need to take you to the doctor?"

"NO, No. I'm fine. Just take me home and Dean can take me if it doesn't stop. But I want to. I have to make sure he is ok first." Bethany helps me back to the car as the pain starts to subside a little. Bethany wasted no time finding every back street and short cut to make it home quickly.

"There's Dean's car." Both of us say as we pull in the driveway. Dean's Camaro is parked in the drive and is still wet from where it looks like he's been washing and detailing it. The driver side door is open and the front door to the house is open.

"Let's call the police, I have a bad feeling about this." Bethany is eager to get the police involved but I'm not. Some of them still don't like Dean.

"Let's go check, maybe he forgot something inside."
We make our way to the front door and start walking
through. "OH MY GOD!" I scream out as I see
Dean's lifeless body lying on the cold tile floor.

Bethany grabs her phone and starts pushing on the
screen to dial 911. As the number starts ringing
through a hand grabs the phone and throws it across
the floor.

"No, no, no. We don't need any more guests at this
party."

Dean

The girls just left for the day and the house is all mine. I'm ready to do nothing and go nowhere. I already called Detective Moore and told him I wanted him to be my best man. He and Angelica have known each other a long time and I think she would like to see him standing beside me at the altar. I ordered my tux the other day and now everything is being delivered to the house. Catering companies from all around are bringing new shit every hour. I lost track of where everything went or goes. I grab a Corona and head for the hammock. I left a note on the door that said to bring everything around back and call if anyone needs me.

The breeze is perfect as it whistles in my ear as the water crashes against the shore. I don't remember a time better than this. My parents lived here for a while and I try to remember everything that went on here, but my teenage years are a blur to me. When they died, something died in me. I didn't care who I was or what I did after that. For the first time in a long time, I feel happy. I have Angelica to thank for that. Thinking back on her all these years ago, I wonder what she saw in the punk teenager. I hated this place and hated that it took all my parents' time away from me, so I wanted nothing to do with anyone that worked here or had family here. When my parents died, I blamed everyone that had any dealings with them. I never did blame Angelica though. I always wished I had talked to her sooner but I was afraid she wouldn't like me. I wanted them back and I wished that everyone else died instead. I couldn't hide my pain very well and I was kicked out of the boy's home and foster care time and time again. I lost my virginity to Roxanna and she was an amazing woman.

After a while the sex began to get old and the girls all felt the same. There was no emotional satisfaction for me anymore. I wanted to get to know someone and take them on a date and not just fuck them and leave them for the next set of tits that where flashed my way.

Gabriela made me feel something that I had never felt before. I had no clue that she was drugging me and that I didn't feel anything for her, but just for the toxin running through my veins. The first day I saw Angelica, I felt something real and it scared the shit out of me. I've never felt that way before and I didn't know what to do. When Angelica looked into my eyes, I knew she was the one. She was the one that was pulling me out of the deep, dark hole that I have been living in. I knew she was going to save me.

The last of the decorations are delivered and the house is finally quite once again. Angelica and Bethany have been gone the better part of the day and I hope they are having fun. I don't know what the hell they are doing but I think they both needed a day out of the house. I know Angelica has been feeling bad the past few days and even though she never said anything to me about it, I've seen it on her face. Her ankles are swelling and I watched her holding her side from time to time. She still has a month before her due date, but I figure with her small size, she might go early and that scares the hell out of me. I can't believe that I am about to marry the woman I love and then we're going to have a baby.

My phone vibrates and I pull it out of my pocket to see who it is.

Bethany: Angelica just passed out at the hair salon. Adam and Arron checked her out. They think she's fine but she doesn't want to go to the hospital. We are at Carl's by the bay.

Oh, my God. My heart sinks. Is she ok? Is she going

into labor? I grab my keys and wallet and head out to the car. I'm going to head over to Carl's. It's not far away and I'm not going to stop for anything until I get there. I head out the front door to the car and open the door. There is still water on the hood from where I washed it earlier and was letting it air dry. I hate seeing water spots on the car but I really didn't want to take the time to dry it off by hand. I feel a sharp pain in my head and I fall face first into the car.

"What the fuck?" I yell as I turn around to see Dave standing behind me with a baseball bat and he has it pulled back for another swing. I push off the car and hit him in the stomach with my shoulder and drive him to the ground.

"No one is going to pull me off you this time." I scream as my knuckles make contact with his face. Blood is spewing from his lip and nose and Dave is laughing at me.

"Get off me you little bitch." He puts one leg under my chest and pushes me off his body and I fall back into the car. Before I push myself back up, he connects his small fist to my chin and my head hits the side of the car. I see Dave running toward the house as I shake off the last blow to my face.

"Get your ass back here." I give chase and tackle him in the foyer. We both crash to the ground, but to my surprise, he springs back to his feet. His knee catches me in the forehead as I try to stand up. The force sends me up right and I counter with an uppercut to his jaw. Blood once again flies from his mouth and hits the wall behind him. I haven't been in too many fights growing up, but I have taken boxing classes to help keep my body in good shape. I understand how to stick and move and my instructors always told me that I had a natural ability to evade punches. Today though, Dave is able to land most if not all of his punches and I can't seem to evade him very easily. Every time one of my fists makes contact with his weasel head, he's able to counter and use my head as a punching bag as well. The guy knows how to fight and he isn't holding anything back this time.

The harder I fight the more precise Dave's punches to my face and temple are. He isn't trying to hurt me. He's trying to knock me out for some reason. I don't know what he's planning to do, but I'm not going to let him get the upper hand.

"Come on Dean, you're slowing down." Dave mocks me as he circles me in our makeshift boxing ring. A sinister grin shines across his face and I know he is finding this entertaining. He throws another punch toward my head and I duck out of the way and land a hard elbow into his side. I feel one if not two rips break under the force of my elbow and Dave screams out in pain. Before I can attack again my cell phone rings and I know it's Bethany or Angelica calling. I don't want them to come home to this, they don't need to see the bloody fight that is taking place and if Dave does knock me out, there is no telling what that sick motherfucker will do to them. I run toward my phone to answer it and tell them not to come home but before I am able to answer the phone, Dave wraps his sweaty arms around my waist dragging me to the ground. The phone falls and answers but drops the call right away. I struggle to break free and the phone starts ringing again.

Just as I feel Dave's grip begin to loosen and I know I can break free, I feel another sharp pain in my head. This time it sends me to the ground.

"What the hell took you so long?" Dave says as he pushes himself off my limp body. Through the sweat and blood, I see Gloria standing over me with the ball bat in hand. She's laughing at the display of aggression she just witnessed. I reach over to answer the phone and have it by one hand as I try to slide the answer bar over. I don't know if it answers or not.

"I wanted to see if you could really bet him." She says as she turns toward Dave with a smile.

"You stupid, BITCH. I will kill both of you." My threat is laughed off as Dave walks over to my head. He raises his foot in the air over my face.

"Night, night. I'll make sure I take good care of your

bitch when she gets here." Before I can move and try to fight anymore he slams his foot down on my head and everything goes black.

My head is killing me as I wake up laying on the floor face down. Blood is still coming out of my nose and lip and when I try to pull my head up from the cold tile floor, I stick to it a little as the blood around me has begun to dry. I groan and move, hoping that Dave or Gloria isn't standing near me, ready to use that ball bat once more.

"Help me, Please, God. Help." I can hear Bethany's voice in the other room. I can't tell if she is on the phone or if she is yelling at someone else. I push my body off the floor and ready myself for the next round of fighting. I know this time I can't go down and I might even have to fight dirty.

"I'm at Sapphire Coast at the Beach house of Angelica Muller's." Good, it sounds like she is on the phone with the police. If she can stay hidden long enough where she's at, maybe help will be on the way.

"Who are you calling you whore, give me that fucking phone." My body tenses as I hear Dave's voice yelling at her. That sick bastard is going to hurt or kill her. Then my heart sinks even more, where is Angelica. NO.

"ANGELICA!" I scream as I get to my feet and stager toward the sound of the voices. My energy is depleting and I can't seem to shuffle my feet fast enough.

"No, no! Stop! Stop!" Bethany's voice strains as she fights with Dave I presume.

"Bang!" Oh, my God. My heart stops and I stiffen where I stand.

"I told you what would happen. Did you really think Dean could insult me like that and I wouldn't come back for him?" Dave's voice bounces off the walls in the house and hits me harder than his fist did.

"Help me, please help me." Bethany keeps screaming and I hear someone approaching from behind me. I turn to see Gloria holding the ball bat above her head and she is running full speed at me. Her eyes are red and intense as she quickly approaches. I brace myself for another blow from her ruthless bat and I hold one arm to try to block the blow. I'm too weak to move and I know that I have to save what energy I have for Dave. As she closes the gap between us a flash appears behind her. Then I hear the sound of a gunshot.

"Bang." Then another flash. "Bang."

Gloria falls feet from me and her back fills with

blood. Who the hell just shot her and are they going to do the same to me?

"Dean, you ok?" Detective Moore comes into the light holding his Sig, sweeping the corners as he makes his way toward me. Before I can answer him if I'm ok he pushes past me toward the sound of other voices in the house. "Where's Angelica?"

I nod toward the other room and he wraps an arm under me as he helps me toward the door.

"Please don't let me die. I don't want to die. Please." Bethany is crying as we both hear Angelica's voice.

"No, stay away. No!"

"We started a game and I never got to finish. There's no one to stop me now." Dave is walking toward Angelica as we come into the room. Angelica is laying on the floor and her face is bleeding from what looks like Dave's fist. My veins turn cold and every muscle in my body tightens as I get my feet back under me. Dave attacks again, pinning Angelica down to the floor and he starts to choke the life out of her. She moves her legs under him and pushes him off once, but he is too strong and is back on her again. He punches her in the face once, then twice. My bones are stiff and my hatred for this sick bastard has boiled to the top.

"GET OFF MY SISTER!" Bethany tackles Dave off Angelica and tries her best to stop his attacks but he throws her like she is a fly off his back and he is back on Angelica. He tears her clothes and rips her shorts off her bloody body.

"Let's see someone stop me now." He hits her again in the face and her body becomes limp. Detective Moore is holding his gun up and I'm shaking my head at him.

"You might hit Angelica." He shakes his head and narrows his sights on the bastard that is attacking the love of my life. His finger pulls the trigger as he steadies his body. I push off him and run toward Dave with what energy I have left. I'm not willing to take a chance of him hitting Angelica. The force of me running throws Detective Moore's stance off and his arm goes up, discharging his weapon in the ceiling. Dave turns to see me running full speed at him and he raises his hands, trying to brace himself for what is about to come. I don't know where my strength comes from but I know it isn't going to last long.

My fist makes contact with his face and then my knee lands on his rips that I broke earlier. He screams out in pain and that infuriates me even more. I hit him again and again in the face and I feel my knuckles begin to split open from the countless blows. Dave smiles at me as I think of nothing more than his head splitting open and me killing this sick bastard once and for all.

"Dean!" I hear Detective Moore scream at me and I turn to see him holding Angelica's head up off the ground. She begins to come to and I hit Dave one last time in the face, sending blood across the floor along with his front teeth.

"Is she ok?" I yell as I shove Dave to the ground and use his body to force myself to my feet.

"Pumpkin? Pumpkin? Are you ok?" Detective Moore says holding her tight to his chest. My eyes grow wide as I notice the affection that he is showing her. It's more than just one of concern, but more of love.

"Pumpkin?" I say just as he turns to me. He isn't looking at me but rather past me at Dave. He sets Angelica's head back to the ground and stands up, walking past me to stand over Dave.

"You can't do shit to me. You're a fucking pig." Dave holds his hands out, fist together. "Arrest me, officer." With a smug grin, he laughs at Detective Moore.

"FUCK YOU!" Detective Moore pulls his gun out and aims it at Dave's head. His smile fades as the flash, followed by a loud bang finds its mark. Dave's head falls back to the floor and Detective Moore lowers his weapon to Dave's chest and fires until clicking noises are heard from his service weapon running out of bullets.

Dean

"Everyone freeze." I hear men running into the house and radios squelching. I turn to see a dozen officers with guns drawn, yelling commands to all of us. Bethany holds her hands up and lays flat on the ground as she is told too. She has blood coming from mouth and head. Detective Moore drops his gun and identifies himself as an Orlando Detective. When the attention is turned to me, I don't move. I'm holding Angelica in my arms and began to cry.

"I said get the fuck on the ground." One of the officer's yells, still with his weapon pointed at my head.

"Fuck off!" I look up at him and he still doesn't move. "FUCK! OFF!" I yell again, this time pushing his gun out of my face.

"H-He's with me. He's with me. Lower your weapons." Detective Moore says as he runs to my side.

"She needs an Ambulance, now." I tell him. He doesn't move as he bends down next to her. He begins to cry like I am doing as he looks at Angelica's beaten body. "HEY! She needs an AMBULANCE! NOW!" I yell again. This time looking at the officer I told to fuck off just a second ago. He nods and speaks into his mic. Less than a minute later, Adam and Arron come running into the room.

"Dean, watch out, we've got her." They lift her body as gently as they can onto the stretch and then both brother's faces turn white.

"WHAT?" I yell. Trying to force myself up to my feet.

"She's bleeding."

"No shit, she just got the piss beat out her."

"No, she's bleeding lower."

Detective Moore and I look down between her legs and notice a pool of bright red blood forming on the stretcher.

"Oh my God." I drop to my knees and began to cry. "NO! NO! It can't be." I beg and plead that this is just a bad dream and that I'll wake up with Angelica next to me and everything will be normal. She can't be lying in her own blood. I want our baby to still be kicking, waiting to come out.

"Come on guys, we'll escort you to the hospital." One of the officers says as they help Adam and Arron out of the house and to the Ambulance.

"Come on Dean, I'll take you and Bethany to the

hospital. You need to get checked out as well." I don't move, but I feel Detective Moore pull me to my feet.

"You can't leave. We have a ton of questions for all of you." The officer that held his gun for so long at my head says as we start our way toward the front door. "Are you listening to me? Stop!" He yells again, but his threats fall on deaf ears.

"Move aside." Detective Moore says as we get closer to the front door. I see two police cars pull off and then Ambulance. Behind them two more police cars follow. Their sirens are deafening as they pull out onto the main road and scream toward the hospital.

"You're not leaving until we find out what the hell happened here. We have a dead body in there." The little prick says again, pushing Detective Moore in the chest.

Detective Moore grabs the officer by the shirt and pulls him off the ground. With at least a good foot of height on the little officer and one hundred if not more pounds on him, Detective Moore lowers his eyes to meet the little prick's face. "You will step aside while we go to the hospital and make sure the woman we love is ok. You can follow us there if you want and take statements in the waiting room. But I will be **damned** if you are going to stand in the way of me or anyone else from seeing her. Do I make myself perfectly clear?"

The officer's eyes grow wide as the threat sinks in and he can tell that Detective Moore isn't making an empty threat. If the officer doesn't move, he is going to relieve him of his duties, for a while.

"That's fine. We'll meet you at the hospital." The officer agrees as Detective Moore sets him back on the ground. My head's still spinning and I can't see straight , let alone even walk. I motion to my car, which isn't being blocked in by all the police cars, and fall into the passenger seat as Bethany climbs in the back. Detective Moore starts the car and shoves it into first gear, releasing the clutch as he spins and slides out of the drive toward the hospital. A police car pulls out behind us and tries to keep up, but is soon left behind. The Camaro rockets through the street at triple digit numbers. Detective Moore turns on my red lights and siren but they can't even keep up with his speed. He isn't stopping for red lights or oncoming cars. Nothing is getting in his way. On straight stretches, he is pushing the car to one fifty plus.

"What did you mean, the woman we love?" I look at Detective Moore waiting for a response but he smiles as he thinks back on his words.

"She still hasn't told you? Has she?"

"Told me what? What are you talking about?"

"I love her. I have for a while. I even asked her to marry me. We had been seeing each other for a few months and when I saw the way she looked at you the day your car exploded, I knew I had to do something. I figured I had to act fast, or I was going to lose her." He shakes his head and looks over at me with a tear in his eye. "But. She never answered me. That's when I knew she loved you. She always has."

My heart sinks in my chest and I close my eyes. This must be a bad dream, there is no way the woman I love, the woman I'm going to marry in two days, and the woman that is carrying my baby, *might* be in love with someone else? Or at least, someone else is still in love with her.

ABOUT THE AUTHOR

My name is Nathan K Fulkerson. I live in Kentucky with my beautiful and loving wife, Kristin, and I am blessed with two great daughters, Karlie and Kaylie. I have fallen in love with writing and have been writing since 2014. I have published four other books on Amazon but this is my first novel. I love writing and am ready to keep sharing my works. Thank you for reading and don't forget to check out my other books as well.

Made in the USA
Middletown, DE
04 March 2022